To T,

Happy Reading.

Stephen Ainley was born in Birmingham in 1952. He served in the British Airborne in the 1970s, before emigrating to Australia. He wrote many articles and short stories before having his first novel, *The Dennis Bisskit Adventures*, published in 2017. He resides in Western Australia with wife, Jane, and Irish Terrier, O'Malley.

Dedicated to my beautiful wife, Jane, who has always encouraged me to be silly.

Stephen Ainley

Dennis Bisskit and the Man from Paris with the Very Large Head

AUSTIN MACAULEY PUBLISHERS™

LONDON • CAMBRIDGE • NEW YORK • SHARJAH

A CIP catalogue record for this title is available from the British Library.

ISBN 9781788784832 (Paperback)
ISBN 9781788784849 (Hardback)
ISBN 9781788784856 (E-Book)

www.austinmacauley.com

First Published (2018)
Austin Macauley Publishers Ltd
25 Canada Square
Canary Wharf
London
E14 5LQ

Part 1

March 1969

Dennis glanced at his watch again and then stared into the gloom. "We'll give it ten more minutes," he told Stinky. Then, despite the cold wind, he wound the window down a bit further and added, "You do know, they have invented this new thing called deodorant." Stinky ignored him, so he continued, "Yankee invention I think, evidently very useful for when you're cooped up for hours in a small car with someone who's still wearing the same socks they wore at school."

Stinky smiled, folded up the newspaper he'd been reading and threw it into the back seat. "As usual, you are slightly exaggerating, Ginge, I bought these socks on the day I left school, so that's only…" He screwed up his eyes and thought for a moment, "Wow, it's about seven years ago, I can't believe it's that long." Dennis wound the window down as far as it could go and muttered, "Time flies when you're enjoying yourself."

He glanced over and saw that Stinky was using a hand to brush back his unruly hair. Not for the first time he felt a pang of jealousy. He looked up at his own reflection in the rear-view mirror. Many years ago, someone had told him that the best thing about having ginger hair was that you rarely went bald. I must be one of the rare ones, he thought to himself. Funnily enough, he'd always been very happy with short hair when he was growing up; everyone had short hair. When he'd joined the army in 1963, he hadn't even required a short haircut, because he already had one. But then suddenly, everything had changed. He'd gone home on leave one day to find the world had gone mad. Young lads of Dennis's age were walking around with hair down to their collars, and it had only got worse. For years, he'd complained about 'the falling standards' and 'the moral decline of the empire', in fact, long hair was blamed for most of the world's problems. But slowly, as he neared the time when he would leave the army, he started imagining himself with long hair. After initially telling everyone that The Beatles would be forgotten about in a matter of months, he'd finally come to like their music. Sometimes, when he was having a shave, and no one was around, he'd stare at his reflection in the mirror and imagine himself with long hair. He thought that maybe he could buy some of those glasses with the round lens, and he'd look like a ginger, John Lennon. But unfortunately, this wasn't to be. As soon as he'd left the military and started growing his hair, he'd realised to his horror, that for the last few years, whilst he'd been doing his bit to prevent the moral decline of the British Empire by sticking to his short back and sides, he'd actually been losing his hair and hadn't noticed. At this point of time, he had grown it longish, but very carefully combed and stuck down, and that was all well and good whilst he was inside and out of the wind. Of course, he shouldn't have been surprised. His granddad was bald, and his father was bald. It was okay for his granddad, he was in his 70s now and it was socially acceptable to be bald in your 70s, and his father had always been bald as far as Dennis knew. He'd been born bald, and had just carried on with it. He'd found the perfect method to avoid losing hair, he'd just not bothered having any in the first place. Only recently his father had studied Dennis's scalp and proudly announced, "I'd say you have about two years and you'll look just like me," as if he were passing on some sort of prized gift. It's okay for him, Dennis thought, but here I am in the Swinging 60s, when hair has never been so important, and I'm having to hang on to whatever I've got left every time the wind blows.

"Penny for your thoughts—" he looked up, Stinky was staring at him.

"Oh nothing," Dennis told him, "I was just thinking we may as well call it a night, no one's coming."

He started the engine and drove off slowly down the road. Stinky leaned forward, picked up a card from on top of the dashboard and read it out aloud.

"BISSKIT AND BLACKSHAW, PRIVATE INVESTIGATORS." Then he turned to Dennis and said, "I still don't see why your name had to come first." His friend carefully shook his head so as not to disrupt his hair.

"I've explained it before; it's just alphabetical, Stinky. Bisskit comes before Blackshaw. Anyway, it sounds more distinguished." Stinky still wasn't happy.

"Well, what about, DOUBLE B PRIVATE INVESTIGATORS, that sounds good."

Dennis pretended to give it deep thought, but eventually said, "No. Double B sounds too much like a bra size; I think we should stick with what we've got."

At the bottom of the card, under their names, it read, "NO JOB TOO SMALL".

It's just as well, Stinky thought to himself, because small jobs are the only jobs we seem to get. A gust of wind came through the open window, and Dennis's carefully combed hair unwound, and flapped about above his head, like a swarm of angry, ginger bees. The car swerved slightly as he struggled to close the window with one hand, hold down his hair with the other, and steer the car with his knees.

Stinky pretended not to notice.

Dennis pulled up near his friend's house and watched him open his front gate. "See you at eight," Dennis shouted.

Stinky turned back. "Eight? Remember I have a life Ginge, and as far as I know, we don't have any urgent business going on."

"Okay," Dennis told him, "let's make it nine." He watched as his old friend walked towards his house. A light was on and he saw the curtain move. Of course, Stinky had a life. His wife Brenda would be sitting up waiting for him, probably with his supper and a hot drink, all prepared.

He blew the car horn and drove off. A year or so back, when they were home on leave from the army. Stinky had quite by chance bumped into Brenda Rumble, whilst buying a newspaper. They had gone out together a few times years earlier when Stinky and Dennis had been in the Scouts but had then lost touch. Four months later, on their next leave, they were married, and Dennis was Best Man. Of course, Stinky had wanted his friend as Best Man, but he was also concerned about the speech. He knew that his friend loved to be centre stage and was worried that the speech would be all about Dennis. His concerns had grown as the wedding day got closer, especially when he'd spotted his friend carrying a huge notebook around, which he'd been told, contained the first fifteen drafts of the speech.

"Slowly getting there," Dennis had said.

As it had turned out, Stinky needn't have been concerned. Almost inevitably, a disaster had occurred, which meant that no one had got to hear the huge speech.

A few minutes later, Dennis pulled up outside his mum and dad's house. Unlike Stinky's home, there were no welcoming lights on here. He sat there for a while staring into space.

"I've really got to get my own place," he muttered sadly to himself. He opened the door and climbed out into the cold night. As he walked towards the house, he suddenly felt a twinge and rubbed where the pain had come from.

"The old war wound," he mumbled. That's what he liked to call it if people asked. He suddenly stopped in his tracks. He couldn't believe it; he was turning into his father. His dad had a scar on his forehead, there since World War Two, that he still referred to as an old war wound, received on a secret mission. Of course, it had turned out that it really had been caused by a flying beer bottle, hitting him on the head whilst he was lurking in a doorway.

"It's true," he muttered again, "I'm turning into my dad, I'm losing my hair, and I have a pretend war wound." He sadly opened the front door and entered the cold house.

Chapter 1
12 Months Earlier

In the mid-1960s, the Staffordshire Regiment had left their spiritual home of Whittington Barracks, in Lichfield, and had been posted to Connaught Barracks, Dover, a military camp with a long history and a great view over The English Channel.

One Saturday morning, Dennis Bisskit sat down on a bench overlooking the choppy sea and watched a ferry slowly making its way towards France. He smiled to himself as he remembered the day they had arrived at the camp. They had paraded on the large square and soon heard the familiar 'clip, clop' of Colour Sergeant Plunkett, marching towards them. The sun glinting off his boots, buckles and teeth. He had stood in front of them for several minutes without speaking. Dennis could sense the fear in some of the newer recruits. He was an old hand now, with five years' service and several tours overseas behind him, but even so, he still tried to avoid Buckethead, as he was known, as much as he possibly could.

Suddenly the Colour Sergeant screamed, "Stand at ease," and several hundred right feet crashed down onto the tarmac, hands shot behind backs. Buckethead, stared with contempt obviously not happy about something, but eventually screamed, "Stand easy," and rows of soldiers relaxed slightly. He suddenly turned and pointed into the distance.

"Look at that view, lads," he shouted, but not quite as loudly as usual. "The White Cliffs of Dover, The English Channel. It's what keeps us apart from them." He didn't say who exactly, but Dennis suspected that he meant the rest of Europe.

"I know what some of you are thinking. You are worried, you probably cannot sleep for worrying, you are thinking, how will we ever manage here in Dover, so far away from Planet Plunkett. Well, I can set your minds at rest lads, you have no reason to fear. Because I am here and where I am, so is Planet Plunkett." He tapped the tarmac with his pacing stick, just to emphasise the point.

"Hear that sound, lads?" he shouted manically, "that is the sound of Planet Plunkett."

Buckethead looked around, and Dennis was horrified when he glanced in his direction, and then his eyes moved along the row and settled on Stinky.

"Some of you who have been around awhile, like Corporal Blackshaw and Lance Corporal Bisskit, know exactly what I mean." His eyes moved back to Dennis, who for some reason felt the need to nod in the affirmative, even though actually, he had no idea what Buckethead was talking about. "We have travelled to lands far away, wild lands, dangerous lands, lands where it's virtually impossible to get a decent cup of tea, but do you know what, lads?" he asked. One of the newer lads, Private Crumpet, foolishly interrupted and asked, "What, Colour Sergeant?" obviously not yet knowing that when Buckethead asked a question, he did not like to be interrupted with an answer. Whilst Crumpet contemplated the error of his ways by doing twenty push-ups, Buckethead continued, "The point I'm trying to make, lads, is…" *Thank God for that,* Dennis thought, we are finally getting to the point. "The point is, wherever we are, it doesn't matter where it is, there is always a little bit of Planet Plunkett with us, to keep you all cocooned and feeling safe." He sounded almost emotional, and it came as no surprise to Dennis when he suddenly shouted, "Don't just stand there, lads, get down and say hello to Planet Plunkett, give me twenty of your best."

Crumpet, who had only just staggered to his feet, reluctantly dropped back down again. He glanced over at Dennis and gasped, "Is he mad?"

"Oh yes," Dennis assured him, "stark raving bonkers."

Dennis heard footsteps, turned and saw his best friend, Stinky Blackshaw, approaching. As usual, he looked immaculate. Before they had joined the army, it had always been Dennis who took charge of things; Stinky seemed happy just to follow along. But, immediately they joined up, it was as if Stinky had found his vocation in life. He had taken to military life like a duck to water. He was already a full Corporal, and there was talk that he could be promoted to Sergeant before too much longer. Meanwhile, Dennis, who had seemed like a natural leader all those years back in the Boy Scouts, had struggled from day one.

He had remained a Private for five years, in fact, there had been occasions when he would have been reduced to something even lower than a Private if there had been such a thing. A couple of months earlier, mainly due to several experienced soldiers leaving the army all at the same time, he had been promoted to Lance Corporal, but as Buckethead had kindly pointed out, "Don't think for one minute that this means you're a good soldier, Bisskit, because, in reality, you are a rubbish soldier. No, what this means is that we are so desperate, you are all we have left, and if I was you, I would make the most of this opportunity, because in a few weeks, some of the new recruits, lads who have only just discovered the joys of Planet Plunkett, will have surpassed the sum knowledge of all you have managed to acquire in the last five years, and when that day arrives, I may think to myself, 'Do we really want Bisskit as a Lance Corporal, when we could promote a new lad, a young lad, a lad who truly understands the workings of Planet Plunkett'?." Then he had presented Dennis with his Lance Corporals stripes, told him to make sure he sewed them the right way up and marched off.

Dennis had long since learnt to dismiss Buckethead's speeches instantly, because they were always much the same, whether he was in a good mood or a bad mood. Instead, he was delighted after all this time; he was finally making progress.

Stinky sat down next to him on the bench, "Where have you been?" Dennis asked. "We are wasting valuable weekend time here."

His friend smiled and held up a letter. "I was just reading this letter I got yesterday, it's from a girl."

"Oh I see, that explains the smile on your face. Is it anyone I know?"

Stinky's smile was even wider. "As a matter of fact, you may remember her, Brenda Rumble."

Dennis stared across the English Channel, deep in thought, "That name does ring a bell." he muttered, and then it came to him. "Just a minute, Brenda Rumble, wasn't that the girl you went to see *The Sword of Sherwood Forest* with, many years ago, instead of going with me?"

Now Stinky started laughing. "That's the one. I bumped into her when I was home on leave, hadn't seen her for years. We got along great, Ginge; we've been writing to each other."

Dennis continued staring towards France and finally said, "*The Sword of Sherwood Forest* was a great movie. Nobody plays Robin Hood as good as Richard Greene," and then suddenly added, "How come I'm only hearing about Brenda Rumble now?"

Stinky shook his head and pointed at the stripe on his friend's sleeve. "Because of that. I came back from leave, and I couldn't get a word in, you kept looking at yourself in the mirror. I said, 'Boy have I got big news for you, Ginge,' and you said, 'That's Lance Corporal Ginge, if you don't mind,' and then I said, 'Guess who I met in Dudley?' and you said, 'This is just the start Stinky, another five years and I could be General Sir Dennis Bisskit,' so I just gave up."

Dennis apologised and told his friend he was very happy for him. "I think she could be the one, Ginge."

Stinky told him, "She could be the future Mrs Blackshaw."

Chapter 2
March 1969

Dennis opened the front door and was surprised to see the light on in the front room. He shouted, "Hello, anyone there?" his mother came back with, "In here."

She was sitting in her armchair, brushing his father's top hat. "Hello love," she smiled, "did you have a good night?"

"Not bad, Mum," Dennis told her, "but you know I can't discuss a case," he added. He always said this; it saved him having to tell her just how bad things were going. He noticed his dad's black suit, carefully ironed and folded over the back of a chair.

Mrs Bisskit saw him looking and said, "Big funeral tomorrow, it's for Doctor Jennings. Your dad says he's expecting a huge turnout, so he has to look his best." Dennis nodded, he still couldn't believe it.

For years, his father had worked at Dudley Zoo, mainly cleaning out the elephant enclosure. This had led to many complaints from neighbours about the smell, as he was always bringing home sacks of elephant poo to put on his roses. Dennis had expected him to work at the zoo all his life but had been amazed one day, when he came home on leave from the army and discovered that his dad had packed in his job and was now working for Nutter's Funeral Director's. As he'd explained to Dennis, he had reached as far as he could go in the zoo business; once you've cleaned the elephant enclosure, there's no way you can get any higher, but there would always be people dying. "It's a job with a future," he'd said, and then added, "You like statistics Dennis, well here's one, ten out of ten people will die. It's the job that keeps on giving." And amazingly he seemed to love it. He had now worked his way up to chief undertaker. For big funerals, he would lead the procession, wearing his best funeral suit and top hat.

"I'll just never get used to Dad being an undertaker," Dennis told his mum.

"Well, the money is a lot better, and at least the neighbours are happier, he's not bringing bags of elephant poo home."

"Yes," Dennis laughed, "let's hope he doesn't start bringing his work home with him from this job."

Just then the door opened, and Granddad walked in yawning and scratching his head. He looked up, smiled and shouted, "Eef, eef," whilst pointing at his mouth.

"They are in your mug of cocoa, where you left them," Mrs B. said.

He walked over to the sofa and spotted his half-empty mug on the little table next to it. Reaching in, he pulled out a set of dentures, shook them, put them in his mouth and drank the remains of the cold cocoa. "That's better," he mumbled and then asked, "Do you know where the paper is, I'm going to the toilet, and this could take a while."

Mrs Bisskit pointed to the newspaper and said, "Well, I'm off to bed soon, so I'll see you both in the morning."

He turned to walk off, but Dennis had to ask, "How come you spend so long in the toilet, Granddad? Sometimes you're in there for hours."

His granddad stared at him for a moment and then replied, "You don't need to worry about that, its grown-up stuff."

Dennis couldn't believe it. "I'm twenty-three, I have my own business, I've just spent over five years fighting for my country, just how grown-up do I need to be?"

Granddad relented. "Fair enough," he said, "it's old people's stuff. The thing is, I feel like going a lot, but when I get there, often I don't want to go, but if I go back to bed, just as I'm getting to sleep, I'll want to go again, so I may as well just go, read the paper and wait until I want to go. And now I'm going." He turned and walked out of the room.

"You know," Dennis said to his mother, "I'm none the wiser now, it's very complicated, this getting older business."

His mother got up, kissed him on top of his head and said, "You don't know the half of it, my boy, make the most of this because these are the best years of your life." She told him she'd see him at breakfast time and left him standing in the middle of the room, suddenly, feeling depressed at the thought that here he was; still single, still living with his parents, partner in a business that made no money, losing his hair and discussing toilet problems with his granddad, and evidently, these were the best years of his life.

Chapter 3
12 Months Earlier

The boys sat at a table in the corner of the bar. Several other young lads stood around with drinks in their hands. Even though they were dressed in civilian clothes, it was obvious that they were soldiers. This was 1968 after all; it seemed that everyone under fifty who still had hair was wearing it at least collar length, and lots, much longer than that. Meanwhile on Planet Plunkett, only that morning, Buckethead had accused Dennis of being a hippie, because his sideburns were a quarter of an inch longer than the regulations allowed. "It's the thin end of the wedge," the Colour-Sergeant had told him. "Next thing, you will be wearing a headband and prancing around with flowers in your hair, and then, when I say 'we are off to war, lads' you will say, 'No, Colour Sergeant, I want to make love, not war' well, let me tell you right here and now, Bisskit, the only love we have around here is the love for Planet Plunkett. "Men may well be looking like girls out there," (he pointed towards the rest of the world) "but here," (he tapped the ground) "men will remain men until the day when I say 'it's okay, lads, you may now look like girls' and when do you think that day will come, Bisskit?"
Dennis made a wild guess, "Never, Colour Sergeant."

Buckethead nodded. "Exactly, Bisskit, never; for once you have managed to guess the correct answer, now go and get that hair sorted, you look like a ginger Sheepdog."

"How am I ever going to meet a girl around here?" he said to Stinky. "They can tell we are soldiers a mile off, and they don't like soldiers."

Stinky put down his drink, "Well, you certainly won't meet a girl in here, what we need is a change of pub. When I came into town last week to buy some new shoes, I found a pub called the Britannia, down Townwall Street, looked a bit posh, but I popped in to use their toilet. I couldn't believe it, packed with girls, hardly any blokes in there. We should pop down there tonight."

Dennis wasn't sure. They drank in the Prince Regent every weekend; it seemed disloyal to visit another pub. "We could try," he said eventually, "but as soon as they see we are soldiers, they probably won't want to know us."

Stinky smiled, "Why do they need to know we are soldiers, just invent some other job that they will be more impressed with."

"Like what?" Dennis asked.

"You can be anything you want." His friend told him, "What about a doctor, and then you can say you have to keep your hair short for health reasons."

Dennis wasn't convinced, but after another pint, suddenly said, "Okay, let's give The Britannia a go, tonight."

That evening, Dennis and Stinky dressed a bit smarter than usual and managed to get away from the camp without bumping into their friends. The last thing they wanted was a big crowd of drunken soldiers tagging along with them. They had a few drinks in various pubs that they normally didn't frequent and eventually at 9 pm, walked into The Britannia. Instead of the normal shouting, singing and arguing, that met you when you entered The Prince Regent, they saw a peaceful, brightly painted, lounge bar. It was only about half full, but Dennis could see several unaccompanied girls, drinking and laughing. Through a doorway, he could hear music, he pushed the door open and saw a long-haired man, standing behind a record player. "And now, how about a bit of The Monkees, Daydream Believer," he shouted. He placed a record on the turntable; it made a scratching sound for a few seconds and then suddenly The Monkees were in Dover. A couple of girls ran onto the small dance floor, closely followed by two more, and then a girl dragging her reluctant boyfriend.

Dennis closed the door. "I'm not dancing until I've had a lot more to drink," he told Stinky.

His friend chuckled and shook his head. "And this from the man who once described himself as the Fred Astaire of Dudley."

Dennis walked over to the bar, ordered two pints of beer, turned to his friend and said, "That was many years ago before

I had all my dancing ability knocked out of me on Planet Plunkett."

They had a couple of drinks and then went into the other bar to listen to the music. Engelbert Humperdinck was imploring someone to save him the last waltz. A tall, young lad was doing some sort of slow dance with a short blonde girl. He leaned down and whispered in her ear, she punched him in the shoulder and then giggled. Stinky suddenly tapped Dennis on his shoulder and nodded towards the corner of the room. An attractive girl with long, dark hair, wearing a pink mini-skirt, sat on her own, staring at the dance floor. "Here's your big chance, Ginge, get over there quick before some other bloke spots her."

Dennis stared in her direction; she was nice looking, maybe he should. But he hesitated. "I never know what to say," he mumbled, "and I'm not up to a dance just yet." Stinky placed his drink down on an empty table and turned to his friend.

"Just say, my name's Dennis, I've injured my leg, so I can't dance, but may I buy you a Babycham." Dennis thought for a moment and then without a word, put his empty glass next to Stinky's and strode across the room, trying to look more confident than he felt. The girl suddenly realised someone was standing in front of her, looked up and saw a young man with short, ginger hair staring down at her.

"Do you want something," she shouted. Dennis tried to remember what Stinky had told him and just as Engelbert suddenly lost interest in the last waltz and the music stopped, shouted, "My name's Babycham and I'm injured; can I buy you a dance?" She just stared at him. Dennis turned and noticed everyone else in the room was also staring at him, everyone except Stinky who was staring at the floor, shaking his head. The long-haired disc jockey ran from behind his turntable and said, "'Ere, what's going on, is he annoying you, Dorothy?"

She shook her head and said, "Don't worry, George, it's just a drunken soldier." Dennis tried to look offended.

"I've never been so insulted in all my life. I have a very serious leg injury, so I'm not allowed to dance. I am not a soldier," he shouted, "I'm a doctor."

The long-haired D.J. stared back at him and eventually said, "So, you're a doctor?"

"I certainly am, one of the finest in the country," Dennis assured him.

"Well, in that case, bugger off and fix your leg." Dennis decided the conversation was over, turned and strode back across the room, suddenly remembering halfway across to limp.

"Well, that went well," Stinky announced.

They decided to go back to the peace and quiet of the lounge room and leaned against the bar as they drank.

"This isn't our world, Stinky, we don't belong here," Dennis spoke sadly, dribbling beer down the front of his shirt. "Let's go back to the Prince Regent. Buckethead was right, there's Planet Plunkett, and then there's the other world, we don't belong in the other world anymore."

Stinky nodded his head. "Perhaps you're right. I'll just pop and use the other world's toilet, and then we will leave." He put down his glass and left Dennis to his thoughts. Dennis gulped down the rest of his pint and turned to follow him but instead walked straight into a young girl. She was just lifting her drink from the bar, and when he walked into her, she spilt it all over the counter.

"Why don't you look where you're going?" she screamed.

Dennis had never felt so embarrassed, "I'm s…sorry," he stammered, "please let me buy you another drink."

She took a white handkerchief from her purse and wiped the drink off her hand, muttering, "Just go away, I don't talk to soldiers." Dennis stared at her; she was the most beautiful creature he had ever seen. She was tall and slim, with short, reddish hair; she looked a bit like Cilla Black. He knew he couldn't just walk away. He tried to remember his cover story, but his mind was just a blank.

Suddenly, he chuckled and said, "Oh you mean this?" He pointed at his hair. "I'm not a soldier." He tried to think of something, anything, and then for some reason, 'and later when he told Stinky about it, he had no idea why it had come into his head he said, "It's just for a role I'm playing, I'm an actor, I'm playing Sir Winston Churchill in a play about his early years; normally I have long hair like Mick Jagger."

She stared at him and then said, "I've never seen Churchill with short, ginger hair, I've only ever seen him bald."

"Well, yes, of course," Dennis replied, "in later years, he went bald, but I am playing him as a young lad; he was very ginger; in fact, his friends used to call him, 'Ginger Churchill'."

She didn't seem certain but eventually said, "Well, I've never met an actor before, you can buy me a glass of wine."

Just then, Stinky joined them at the bar and shouted, "Are you ready?"

She looked at Dennis and said, "Is your friend an actor as well?"

Dennis stared at Stinky, hoping his friend understood, and then said, "Oh, he's not my friend, I just met him at the bar, he's just leaving."

Stinky looked at the girl and then at Dennis. "An actor, you say? You didn't tell me you were an actor; you must tell me where you are appearing, I would love to come to the show."

Dennis's brain had gone blank again. "We are just rehearsing at the moment, but it will be advertised in the newspaper very soon," was all he could come up with.

Stinky finally took the hint. "Well, this pub is okay for you actor types, but personally I'm off to The Prince Regent, it's a bit livelier, I may see you there later." With that, he saluted, turned, and took his leave.

As soon as he had left, Dennis turned to the girl and said, "I think he may be a soldier, he was very uncouth, and I certainly will not be going to the Prince Regent, I've heard it's a very rough pub, frequented by unsavoury types."

She nodded in agreement. "My father says the same thing, he said I must never go in there, he doesn't like soldiers," Dennis ordered fresh drinks; she told him her name was Gloria and accepted his request to join her at a table.

Chapter 4
March 1969

Dennis yawned and poured himself a cup of tea. The door flew open and his father walked in dressed in his best black suit. "Big day today, Dad?" Dennis asked.

"A very sad day, Dennis," his father replied, "Doctor Jennings was a wonderful man, highly respected. Nutter's will do their best to give him a good send-off. By the way, Son, do you know why they are building a fence around the cemetery?"

Dennis did indeed know exactly why. His father had already asked him twice this week, but he knew his dad loved his little undertaker jokes, so he said, "No idea, Dad."

Mr Bisskit was so excited he could barely get the words out. "It's because people are dying to get in," he shouted.

Dennis smiled, "Brilliant, Dad, really funny."

He drove around to Stinky's house and blew the car horn. Eventually, the front door opened and his friend emerged, closely followed by his wife, Brenda. They hugged and kissed for so long that Dennis had to blow the horn again and shout, "Come on, we haven't got all day."

He wanted to get the bad news out of the way as soon as possible. A week earlier, a Mr Bunnings had rung them at the office. He'd suspected that his wife was having an affair. She had been going out every Thursday evening for the last few weeks and had told her husband that she was going to the Bingo with a friend. But his suspicions had been aroused when he spotted a poster advertising the Bingo on Friday nights. He had told Dennis and Stinky that he thought she might be having an affair with an old boyfriend, whilst he was doing shift work. They had spent the previous evening parked outside his house, hoping to catch sight of her.

Unfortunately, Mr Bunnings had called that morning and told Dennis that his wife had just confessed to him that she had in fact been babysitting for their daughter to give her a break. Evidently, the family had had a falling out when she had got pregnant. As a regular churchgoer, Mr Bunnings was horrified at the thought of an unmarried, pregnant girl, living in his house, and despite his wife's pleas, had made her leave.

"The good news is," Dennis said, "the family is now back together." He smiled at Stinky and repeated, "That's good news, isn't it?"

Stinky stared out of the window for a while and then said, "Well, I'm very pleased for them; unfortunately, it doesn't help us, that was the only job we had, I was hoping to drag it out for a week or so."

"He's sending us the two pound he owes us on payday," Dennis mentioned, hoping to cheer his friend up.

But Stinky didn't seem to be in a good mood. "That's wonderful," he told Dennis, "once we take out rent for the office and fuel for the car, I should be able to buy a bottle of milk," he turned to look at Dennis and said, "Look, Ginge, I love being a Private Investigator, but Brenda is starting to get a bit annoyed at me making no money, we can't live on my army savings for much longer."

Dennis was horrified, this was his dream job, he really wanted to make a success of it. "Let's see what today brings, Stinky," he mumbled, "I'm feeling quite confident."

Whilst Dennis drove to their office; Stinky read the morning paper. "Well, it looks like the Yanks are going to land on the moon in July," he told Dennis, who didn't seem impressed.

"Personally, I'll believe it when I see it," he mumbled. Stinky suddenly realised something, "Wow, I've just thought, remember Horace Barnstaple, 'The Professor'? He predicted man would walk on the moon by the end of the '60s. Remember it was on that Scout Camp weekend, at the beginning of the decade?"

Dennis still didn't seem impressed. "Well, it was so obvious, I think I made the same prediction myself," he told his friend.

"No, actually you told The Prof. he was mad, and you predicted that the Davy Crockett hat would replace the Trilby, as the most worn hat in Great Britain. Funnily enough, I don't think

I've seen a Davy Crockett hat or a Trilby since you made that prediction."

Dennis quickly changed the subject. "I forgot to tell you, I saw The Prof. a few weeks back, he was home to visit his mother, he actually is a professor now, so that's something we did manage to predict. He was talking about the origins of the universe; I couldn't understand a word he was talking about. He's still working with that Stephen Hawking chap."

Stinky nodded at his friend. "Oh, you mean the secret drinker."

Dennis shook his head. "No, Horace just thought that because he kept falling over, but it turns out he was actually not very well. The Prof. felt quite bad about it."

They pulled up outside of Mr Plum's, the newsagents. He had been there for years, in fact, many years ago, Dennis had delivered newspapers for him. They strode to the back of the shop and started to walk upstairs. Suddenly, Mr Plum appeared from behind the magazine shelf and shouted, "You haven't forgotten this month's rent, have you lads?" Dennis pretended he hadn't heard and sprinted up the steps, leaving Stinky to explain to Mr Plum that they had been so busy they hadn't managed to get to the bank yet.

As he climbed the stairs, he passed the piece of cardboard, taped to the wall with 'BISSKIT AND BLACKSHAW, PRIVATE INVESTIGATORS, NO JOB TOO SMALL' scribbled on it with a pencil. Not for the first time, he thought they really should do a more professional job, but then he doubted if anyone had even seen the sign yet anyway. Apart from Mr Plum and Brenda, no one else had stepped foot inside the office, even though they had put adverts in the local paper and put a notice in Mr Plum's window.

He managed to climb over the stacks of old newspapers in the corridor and opened the door to their office. Office was probably a slight exaggeration. The room Mr Plum rented them for five pounds a month, wasn't much bigger than the toilet at the far end of the corridor. There wasn't really room for a fancy desk, so they had a small table, a couple of chairs and an old filing cabinet. As Stinky had pointed out, they only really needed the two chairs because if a client entered the room, one of them could pop out and stand in the corridor to make some room.

Dennis was sitting in the chair behind the table, staring at the telephone. On the table was a notebook and pencil, which he kept straightening. Whenever he was out of the room, Stinky would move the pencil ever so slightly so that it wasn't quite parallel to the notebook, then chuckle to himself watching the look on his friend's face when he spotted the pencil, not in its proper position.

"It's no good staring at that phone, Ginge," he said, "it won't make it ring any faster." Then left the office to go and get some milk from the corner shop.

Ten minutes later when he came back in, Stinky noticed that Dennis was leaning back in his chair, he had his feet up on the table and a big smile on his face.

"This is it, I told you today could be the day," he shouted.

Stinky couldn't believe it. "You mean we have a job?" he asked. Dennis tried to take his feet off the table, but the chair fell over backwards, wedging him against the wall. He quickly staggered to his feet and carried on talking as if nothing had happened.

"Not just any job, my friend. I have just had the manager of Hewitt's, the new supermarket, on the phone, they have a pilchard crisis and need our help."

Stinky stared at him. "Pilchard crisis?"

"Yes, indeed, Stinky, eight cans of pilchards have gone missing in the last couple of weeks, it's a complete mystery."

Stinky felt a bit deflated, he had hoped for something slightly more important. "It's not exactly the crime of the century, is it?" he muttered.

But as usual, Dennis saw the glass half full. "It's a crime, my friend. We have to start somewhere. I was just reading where a firm in London, Buttercup, Buttercup and Buttercup, Private Investigators, got mentioned for helping to solve a murder. What do you think of that?"

Stinky rubbed his eyes. "The first thing I think is, what a stupid name, why not call themselves, 'The Buttercup Brothers, Private Investigators'?"

Dennis picked up his chair and sat back down on it. "Well, that would just be silly," he said, "they aren't brothers, in fact, as far as I know; they aren't even related."

Stinky sighed, some days he wished he'd just stayed in bed. "So, what you're saying is, three random men called Buttercup, met and decided to all become Private Investigators. Where did you read this, *The Beano*?"

Dennis thought for a moment and then said, "I can't remember where I read it, but it couldn't have been *The Beano*, I don't read that any more, anyway, you're missing the point, which is, we have a big job. Mr Miggins, the manager, wants me to work undercover, pretend I'm just shopping and keep my eyes open for trouble."

Stinky sat down in the other chair and faced his friend. "Surely it would be better if I did that, with your ginger hair you will stand out a mile."

Dennis smiled. "You should know me better than that my friend, you know I'm a master of disguise, I'll be wearing this," he reached behind the chair and held up a large false beard. "Remember when we went to our fancy-dress party and I went as 'Blackbeard the Pirate'," he put on the beard and then reached down again and produced a pirate's hat, which he placed on his head.

"You don't think that may attract attention," Stinky suggested, "a man shopping in Miggins Supermarket, dressed as a pirate?"

But Dennis's mind was made up. "I don't see why it should; people will just think I'm going to a fancy dress party. Anyway, you don't need to worry about me; I can carry this role off no trouble, they don't call me the Sir Laurence Olivier of Dudley without good reason."

Stinky shook his head. "I'm not so sure about that, remember the last time you tried your hand at being an actor? I seem to recall that didn't work out too well out for you."

Chapter 5
12 Months Earlier

Gloria couldn't stop smiling. "I can't believe I am drinking with a real actor."

Dennis shook his head. "Oh, we are just the same as normal people. Although, obviously more talented," he quickly added. He was amazed, normally he just had no idea what to talk to girls about, but with Gloria, it seemed so easy.

"My father would be impressed," she said, "he's always telling me to meet a nice boy, not one of those uncouth soldiers. He's very protective of me, you know."

"It's quite understandable," Dennis told her, "you're a very attractive girl." She smiled and turned away. Dennis couldn't believe it, normally he would never say something like that to a girl, but just pretending to be someone else made it easy. It was as if they were saying it and not him. He explained to Gloria that she wouldn't have seen him in here before because he usually lived up north, but had been offered huge money to come to Dover and play the role of Sir Winston. When she asked if he had done any movie roles, he replied that he had done several, but they had not been released yet. "I'm even in the running to play Robin Hood in a remake of the Sword of Sherwood Forest," he told her, "I've auditioned for it, and they say my Robin could be the finest of this generation."

It was all going along nicely until she suddenly asked him if he had done any Shakespeare.

Dennis chuckled. "Shakespeare, of course, I've done Shakespeare, every great actor has done Shakespeare." He should then have changed the subject, but by now he had almost convinced himself that he was a great actor.

She put her drink down on the table and leaned towards him. "Oh, please Dennis, please say some words from Romeo and Juliet, it's my favourite."

Dennis almost choked on his pint of mild. "Words, Romeo and Juliet, you want me to say words?" She nodded and looked so excited. He tried to clear his mind. He remembered his English teacher trying to read some Shakespeare to the classroom, many years ago. It was the most boring thing Dennis had ever heard. He had been busy throwing bits of rolled up paper at Stinky's head and hadn't paid much attention. Suddenly, some words came back to him. He cleared his throat, stood up, and said as dramatically as he could, "Romeo, where are you?" He sat back down and noticed she didn't look quite as impressed as he'd hoped. "You mean, O Romeo, Romeo, wherefore art thou," she said, "they're the proper words."

Dennis rubbed his eyes, wishing he hadn't had so much to drink. "Usually. Obviously, we normally say, what you just said, but some nights I like to change it a bit, or else it gets boring if you just say the same thing every night." She still didn't seem convinced, so he quickly stood up and added, "What about another drink?" but before he could leave the table, Gloria said, "What I can't understand is why you would be saying that anyway. Juliet says those lines." Dennis was beginning to wish he had said he was a doctor instead; surely it would have been easier. He smiled down at Gloria. "Well spotted, I wondered if you would notice that. Of course, I only said that the night that the actress playing Juliet was off sick. I had to play both roles. It actually wasn't as easy as you might think, running up and down the steps to that balcony. Still, that's the life of an actor." He quickly turned and walked to the bar before she could ask him anything else.

The rest of the evening, he managed to avoid having to answer any more awkward questions, and as he walked her to the bus stop, she suddenly invited him to her house the next day. She told him her father was working and her mother was away for the day. She wrote an address on a piece of paper, gave him a kiss on the cheek and left him standing at the bus stop with a huge grin on his face.

Chapter 6
March 1969

Dennis moved the two packets of Cornflakes apart and stood on his tiptoes. *Perfect,* he thought. He had a clear view of the pilchard display. He was wearing his pirate's hat, a long black beard, a bright red, frilly pirate's shirt and his frayed, old Boy Scouts shorts. He didn't have any proper pirate's pants but had always felt that his Scouts shorts looked a bit piratey. Mind you, he hadn't tried them on for many years and was surprised to find he'd grown in the last decade. The shorts which had used to be a bit baggy on him were now quite tight and short; in fact, when he looked in the mirror, it looked more like he was wearing his swimming trunks. Still, he didn't have time to get anything else, and all in all, he felt it was a pretty good disguise.

As he tried to look casual whilst keeping an eye on the shoppers, Mrs Jenkins from the fishmongers walked past and said, "Good Morning, Dennis, lovely day, are you off for a swim?" Dennis nodded. Mrs Jenkins was the third person who had said hello to him already. It was bad enough that they recognised him even though he was wearing a pirate's hat, big, black beard, red, frilly shirt and swimming trunks, but what was of greater concern to Dennis was the fact that none of them seemed to think it was unusual.

Towards lunchtime, the supermarket started to fill up. Dennis held a shopping basket in his hand, which he gradually filled up with shopping to look more realistic. His arm was starting to get a bit tired, so he started to put items back on the shelves. He suddenly noticed an elderly man watching him. Dennis nodded, and the man said, "You do realise you are supposed to buy things here and take them home. You don't bring stuff from home and put it on the shelf." Dennis was just trying to think of a good excuse when a voice came over the loudspeaker.

"Will Dennis Bisskit report to the manager's office please, his mother wants a word with him." Dennis couldn't believe it; he had told his mother he was doing vital undercover work at the supermarket. He ignored the message, but a few minutes later he heard the voice again. "If anyone can see Dennis Bisskit, he's the one wearing a pirate's hat, tell him his mother wants a word."

Several people walked around to the aisle he was standing in and shouted, "Dennis, your mother wants you." Everyone stared as he reluctantly made his way to the manager's office. When he opened the door, his mother was chatting to Mr Miggins. She looked up and said. "Oh, there you are Dennis, I just popped in to tell you not to bother getting that corned beef because I'm here now, I can get it." Dennis stared at her with his mouth wide open. "Mum, I'm working undercover, now you have ruined it, everyone knows it's me. In any case, you didn't ask me to get any corned beef."

Mrs Bisskit stood up, folded her arms and shouted, "I know perfectly well that I didn't ask you to get any corned beef, but I thought you might just happen to get some anyway, so I walked all the way around here to get it for you, and this is all the thanks I get." She turned and looked at Mr Miggins who nodded as if he understood it all perfectly. Mrs Bisskit strode towards the office door, shouting, "I'll leave you to your game of pirates. Those shorts look ridiculous by the way; there's a big rip in the back, I can see your underpants. And don't think you're fooling anyone, I have had half a dozen people come up to me and say, 'I've just seen your Dennis in the supermarket dressed as a pirate'," With that, she slammed the door and left.

It was quiet in the office for a moment, and then Dennis said, "Sorry about that, she doesn't understand this undercover work."

Mr Miggins nodded, but as Dennis left, he shouted, "Try and cover up your underpants lad, I know it's the swinging sixties, but our shoppers still aren't ready for that sort of thing."

Chapter 7
12 Months Earlier

Dennis got off the bus at the end of the street and followed the directions on the note, Gloria had given him. He counted off the house numbers, 7, 9, 11 until he reached number 13. "13, unlucky for some," he muttered to himself. He was pleased to see no sign of a car anywhere. Gloria had told him she had the house to herself, but he was still worried. He didn't really want to meet her parents and have to repeat all his acting experiences. He walked up to the front door and was about to knock when it suddenly opened, and Gloria stood in front of him with a big smile on her face. She was wearing a black and white mini dress, with white boots. She looked fantastic.

Earlier that morning, following Stinky's advice, Dennis had crept around to the garden in front of the Officers' Mess and stolen half a dozen red roses, which he had wrapped up in a piece of newspaper. His hands were covered in cuts and grazes, and he still had a couple of thorns in his fingers, but it was well worth it when he saw the look on Gloria's face when he handed them to her.

She blushed and said, "I'll put those in water."

He followed her into the house. "Nice place," Dennis said. "Do your parents own it?"

Gloria came back with the roses in a vase and told him, "No, we are just renting it. We could live at my father's workplace, but he prefers us out of the way."

Dennis noticed that there were still packing boxes in the hallway. "Have you not been here long?" he asked.

Gloria smiled and said, "Not too long. It's hardly worth unpacking anyway. My father moves around a lot with his job. It seems like I haven't seen him much over the years." She looked a bit sad, so Dennis put his hand on her shoulder and said, "That must be terrible. If I ever have children, I'd want to be there for them all the time."

She smiled again as if he'd said the correct thing and led him into a small lounge room. "Wait in here," she told him, "I'm just making some tea and cake." She walked out of the door. This is going well, Dennis said to himself. He looked around the room. It was very neat and tidy as if it wasn't used very much. There was a large sideboard against one wall, and he noticed several photos on a shelf; he walked over to have a look. There were a couple of photos of Gloria, one recent and one, a bit older. Next to this was one of an older lady, unmistakably Gloria's mother and next to that a family photo. Gloria's mother, and then Gloria, and next to her, an older man, obviously her father, with a protective arm around her shoulder.

Dennis opened one eye, he felt dizzy. He was lying on the floor and instantly realised he must have fainted. His legs were shaking as he slowly climbed up off the carpet. From the direction of the kitchen, he heard a voice shout, "Nearly done."

He almost didn't want to look, but he knew he must. He stared at the photo and realised where he was. He was in the eye of the storm. The dead centre of Planet Plunkett. The man with his arm around Gloria was Buckethead. He couldn't believe he had missed all the clues, he thought of all the things she had said. "He doesn't like me talking to soldiers", "My father moves around a lot, with his job", "It's hardly worth unpacking". Then he noticed another photograph he hadn't seen. It showed, Buckethead in uniform receiving some award. Printed at the top of the photo it said, 'Colour Sergeant Norman'... Dennis started giggling hysterically. It almost made it all worthwhile. Suddenly, he heard a car pull into the driveway and a shout from the kitchen, "Oh good; it's Dad, he must have popped home for something. I know he's dying to meet you."

Dennis nearly fainted again; then he ran out of the lounge. He could hear footsteps nearing the door. He looked around him. He heard a key being inserted into the door lock. He sprinted up the stairs, moving faster than he'd ever moved before, and leapt through a doorway, just as a voice shouted, "Hi Gloria, it's Dad."

Chapter 8
March 1969

Dennis pulled his red, frilly shirt out so that it hung over his shorts. His mother had found it for his pirate's costume in a second-hand shop. It was so big that it completely covered his ripped shorts. Now you couldn't see his underpants, but unfortunately, from a distance, it looked like he was wearing a pirate's hat, a long, black beard and a red, frilly dress. He spent the rest of the day wandering around the supermarket, keeping one eye on the pilchard stand but never spotted anyone acting suspiciously. He didn't really mind because the longer the job dragged on, the more money they would make.

Sadly, for their finances, the job only lasted until the following lunchtime.

Dennis was starting to think it was going to be another uneventful day when he spotted an elderly lady lurking near the pilchards. She glanced furtively in all directions before casually placing a tin in her handbag.

Dennis raced down the aisle as fast as he could and slid around the corner. Unfortunately, he forgot that a large display of baked beans had been erected that very morning. Dennis tried to stop but just fell face forward and slid into the display. Dozens of cans of baked beans crashed to the floor, some of them bouncing off Dennis's head. By the time he climbed unsteadily to his feet, the lady was disappearing around the corner of the next aisle. His hat had fallen off, and the false beard had swung around so that it was hanging down the back of his neck. Blood ran down the side of his face, but nothing was going to stop him now. He sprinted around the corner and saw her. He ran, and when he was some distance away, took a flying leap. He landed on the lady's back, and she collapsed to the floor, luckily, landing on top of a stack of toilet rolls. Dennis sat on top of her and pulled her arm up behind her back. Suddenly, he heard Mr Miggins shouting, "What's going on, what are you doing on top of my mother?"

Chapter 9
12 Months Earlier

Dennis closed the door quietly behind him and realised he was in a bathroom. There was a cupboard under the sink but far too small for him to climb into. He heard shouting from a distance, and then closer as if someone were at the bottom of the stairs. "Dennis, Dennis, where are you?"

He opened the window and looked out, it was a fair distance to the ground, but a couple of yards away were branches from a tall tree. He fully opened the window and climbed up so that he was perched on the windowsill. The tree suddenly seemed a long way off, but then he heard Gloria call his name, she seemed a lot closer. He took a flying leap into the unknown.

Colour Sergeant Plunkett had left his daughter searching for her new boyfriend who appeared to have disappeared into thin air. If it was up to him, she wouldn't see boys at all. Still, at least this lad was an actor and not a soldier. He knew only too well what soldiers were like. Mind you, he thought to himself, acting's not a proper job for anyone. He walked around the back of the house toward the shed. He was sure he'd put his rugby boots in there. Hopefully, they weren't buried under all the unopened boxes.

Suddenly, he heard a loud crashing sound coming from above him. He looked up and couldn't believe his eyes. It was like some sort of nightmare. Six feet above his head was Dennis Bisskit. The waistband of his pants had caught on a small branch, pulling them up to his chest. He was just swinging around in the breeze, with tears in his eyes.

Buckethead suddenly remembered what Gloria had called her new boyfriend, DENNIS! Surely not, it couldn't be. Then there was another loud crash, Dennis fell in a heap to the ground. His arch-enemy glared down at him and screamed, "So Bisskit, I hear you are now an actor."

Dennis felt like crying. He slowly got to his feet and stammered, "I was in a play at school, Colour Sergeant."

Buckethead took a step towards him. He was so angry, veins were sticking out of his neck, "You come into my house, the nerve-centre of Planet Plunkett, and attempt to have your wicked way with my daughter, you better not have laid a hand upon her, Bisskit."

Dennis raised his hands in the air as if he were surrendering and quickly shouted, "I never touched her, Colour Sergeant, honestly, she didn't tell me she was your daughter. Obviously, if I had known, I wouldn't have even spoken to her." Buckethead didn't seem convinced; he looked as if he might explode at any moment.

Suddenly, Dennis remembered what he had seen written on the photograph, maybe he had a chance, but did he dare say it? He saw the look on Buckethead's face and blurted it out.

"I'm very sorry, Shirley." The colour drained from the face of the Colour Sergeant.

After a moment he asked, "What did you call me?"

"Shirley. I saw it in your photo, Colour Sergeant, Norman Shirley Plunket.; It's a very unusual name." Dennis said, with more confidence than he felt, and then added, "Well, for a man anyway."

Buckethead's throat had gone dry. He had always feared his unusual middle name getting out. He knew that all his hard-earned respect would vanish. Every time he walked onto the parade ground, there would be wolf whistles and shouts of, "Hello, Shirley".

"It was my father's idea of a joke," he mumbled, "he was a spiteful man." Dennis suddenly felt a bit sorry for him; he seemed almost human. He had visions of a young Buckethead's father standing over him and screaming, "Come on, Shirley, give me twenty push-ups, you're on Planet Plunkett now."

Buckethead took a deep breath and seemed to pull himself together. "This is what is going to happen, Bisskit," he said, in a tone that suggested that it wasn't open to discussion. "You are going to turn around and make your way back to camp, where you are going to forget everything that has happened today, where I live and what my middle name is. More importantly, you are going to forget all about my daughter, her name, what she looks like, everything about her. You are going to avoid drinking anywhere she may be drinking, and if you see her in the street, you are going to run in the opposite direction as quickly as is physically possible. Do you understand me so far?" Before Dennis could answer, he continued, "And for my part, I will also forget this ever happened. It will never be spoken of again, unless, of course, I hear that you haven't kept up your side of the bargain, because if that happens, Bisskit, I shall unleash hell and it won't be a pretty sight. Do you understand?"

A normal person would have just agreed, but Dennis asked, "Is this a career setback for me?"

Buckethead grunted and said, "No, Bisskit, I won't hold this against you in any way. Mainly because I don't need to, since you are such a useless soldier, that is career setback enough."

Dennis decided to get out whilst the going was good, but as he reached the footpath, he quickly glanced back. A sad looking Gloria was leaning out of the bathroom window he had leapt from, she waved and then disappeared.

Chapter 10
March 1969

Stinky couldn't believe it. "Why was his mother stealing pilchards?"

"Well, that's the strange thing," Dennis told him, "she said she was collecting them for her cat, Monty, but evidently, he died three years ago, and then, when her son tried to explain that to her, she asked him if he was Ingrid Bergman. She's not a well woman, Stinky; it's very sad. Still, that's another crime solved."

Stinky shook his head. "Well, it is sad Ginge, but it's also sad for us, I was relying on that job bringing us some money in, more than just a couple of days' worth." Dennis was just trying to think of some way to cheer his friend up when there was a loud banging on the door. They stared at each other. The only person who had ever knocked on the door was Mr Plum, and they knew he was away for the day. Dennis jumped up from his chair.

"Leave this to me," he whispered. As he turned the doorknob and started opening the door, he said in a loud voice, "Good Morning, Bisskit and Black…" that was as far as he got before he recognised the person on the other side of the door.

He was so shocked to see Buckethead that he dropped down to the floor and had done several push-ups before he realised that he was now a civilian. He jumped up and gasped, "Colour Sergeant."

Buckethead said, "Sir."

Dennis said, "You don't have to call me sir, Colour Sergeant."

Buckethead said, "I wouldn't call you sir if you had legally changed your name from Bisskit to Sir. I'm just pointing out that I am not Colour Sergeant any more, I have, finally, got a well-deserved promotion to Warrant Officer, so you can call me sir."

Stinky finally spoke, "Well, we shall certainly call you sir to show respect, but we are not soldiers anymore, and we are not on Planet Plunkett, you are on our planet, so you shall call us Mr Blackshaw and Mr Bisskit."

Dennis had never felt so proud of his friend, but he felt obliged to add, "Or, if you like, you can call me Dennis, sir."

Buckethead stepped further into the room and said, "Let's just stick with Mr Bisskit. No need to pretend we are old friends." He looked around the office and obviously wasn't impressed. "So, this is it, the centre of operations, this is where all the action takes place."

Dennis, who'd had many years of experience ignoring Buckethead's sarcasm, just smiled and said, "Yes, Sir, this is where we do all the planning. Welcome to Bisskit and Blackshaw, Private Investigators."

"And what sort of things do you investigate?" their old adversary enquired.

Stinky started to answer, but Dennis beat him to it. "Oh, anything and everything. Why only this morning we solved a major crime in a supermarket; I apprehended the criminal myself." He touched the cut on his head where he'd been struck by the baked bean can, and added. "I don't mind telling you; she put up quite a fight."

Buckethead was quiet for so long that eventually, Stinky asked, "Was this just a social visit Sir? I thought The Regiment was stationed in Berlin." Without being invited Plunkett sat down on the remaining chair and mumbled, "No, it's good to see you lads, but it's not really a social visit. The Regiment is now in Berlin, but I've been given some leave. The fact is, my daughter, Gloria is missing." He stared at Dennis as he spoke and enquired, "Do you remember her?" Dennis wasn't sure if Buckethead was testing him in some way, so to be on the safe side he said, "Absolutely not, Sir, I didn't even know you had a daughter, and I've certainly never been to your house."

Sir gave a slight nod of approval and then continued.

"She was all set to come to Germany with us, and then on the morning we were due to leave, she just disappeared. I've checked with all her friends; no one has a clue where she is."

Stinky butted in, "With respect, Sir, she's not a child anymore, she may not have wanted to go abroad with you for two years."

Buckethead seemed surprised. "Why would she not want to go to Berlin for two years? Why would she want to be anywhere else than with her mother and me.?"

"Well, it would probably be a bit boring," Stinky said, "I mean she wasn't even allowed to talk to soldiers."

Buckethead looked at Dennis and then back at Stinky, "Who told you that?"

Stinky quickly said, "Nobody, I'm just assuming that would be the case."

To change the subject, Dennis asked if he had reported it to the police, and he told them that he had, but they hadn't shown much interest. They spent another ten minutes discussing Gloria, her interests, friends, their last address and many other things. He agreed immediately with their fees and gave them a contact number where he could be reached.

Surprisingly, he shook their hands and said, "The army is the second most important thing in the world to me, only my family comes above it. Do your best lads." He stood up and in a low voice said to Dennis, "So you never said anything about that day."

Dennis swallowed and said, "Of course not, Sir."

Buckethead hesitated and then added, "What about that other thing, my middle name, did you keep quiet about that?"

Dennis tried to look suitably offended as he replied, "Now look, Sir, I know we had our ups and downs, but my word is my bond, my lips were and still are sealed."

Plunkett gave a slight nod and asked, "How's the old war wound by the way?"

Dennis muttered, "Fine Sir, just the occasional twinge," as Buckethead walked to the door.

Just as he reached it, Stinky said, "We will do our best, Shirley, I mean, Sir."

Buckethead turned to shout at Dennis, but he was already hiding behind his table, so the soldier just walked out and slammed the door behind him.

Dennis slowly arose from behind the table and shouted, "You couldn't help yourself could you, you just had to say it."

Chapter 11
12 Months Earlier

Dennis hadn't bothered hanging around for the bus; he had just run the four miles back to camp as fast as he could. Just in case, Buckethead suddenly had a change of mind and came after him. When he got back, he was soaked in sweat and couldn't stop shaking. He filled a washbasin with cold water and stuck his head under until he had to come up for air. He stared in the mirror as the water dripped off his face. Suddenly, the door flew open and Stinky strode in. "I thought I saw you running up the road, how did it go?"

Dennis just shook his head and then said, "I don't want to talk about it, Stinky. In fact, I'm not allowed to talk about it, so there's absolutely no point in you asking me about it."

Stinky stared at his friend for several minutes and then smiled. "You know you will tell me eventually, Ginge. You know it and I know it, so why waste time, you may as well just tell me now."

Dennis held out for about ten seconds and then said, "You will never guess what Buckethead's middle name is."

Chapter 12
March 1969

"What's in the bag?" Stinky asked, pointing at the carrier bag on the floor. Dennis picked it up and threw it into the corner of their office.

"Just my old Pirate's outfit, don't suppose I'll be needing that again."

Stinky stared at the bag and visibly shuddered.

"I'm surprised you'd even kept it, I mean…you know…the old war wound. Does it still hurt?"

Without thinking, Dennis reached behind him and felt the scar through his trousers.

"Not so bad, it just aches a bit on a cold day," he muttered. "Still, it could have been so much worse."

SEPTEMBER, 1968

The Regiment had finished their posting to Dover and returned to their home at Whittington Barracks, Lichfield. The lads had originally signed on for six years and decisions had to be made to either sign on again or leave. Dennis's mind had been made up for a while now. Even though there was much he had enjoyed about the last few years; he had realised from the very first day that he commenced Basic Training, that he'd made a bit of a mistake. Army life wasn't really for him. There were plenty of things that he was good at, but even he knew that being a soldier wasn't one of them. Not only that, but he knew, despite Buckethead's promises about not holding The Gloria Incident against him, that he was going to be spending the rest of his military career paying for it. He had done more guard duties than anyone else and seemed to find himself being volunteered for every dirty job that came along. No, Dennis had other plans.

It had come to him one day whilst reading one of his favourite books, Sam Spade, Private Investigator.

It had suddenly occurred to Dennis that there was a great need for Private Investigators in Dudley. There seemed to be plenty of them in America, and yet for some reason, the people of Dudley were expected to get by without one.

Obviously, as soon as he came up with the idea, he'd tried to convince Stinky to join him in the scheme. At first, his friend had said it was one of the most stupid ideas that Dennis had ever come up with and that he'd be signing on for another six years.

Dennis wasn't really surprised by this as he knew that his friend felt completely different about the army than he did. He loved the life and was well respected in the regiment, so much so that there were rumours about him being promoted to sergeant before too long. Not only that, he'd now married Brenda and felt that the army provided him with a secure future.

Everything had suddenly changed in August.

First, an influential officer had for some reason taken a dislike to Stinky. Next thing they knew, another soldier had been promoted to sergeant, one much less well-qualified than Stinky, but one who happened to be a cousin of the influential officer. Then Brenda had started to get a bit restless about how little she saw of him. The Regiment had been away on several exercises lately. Stinky had tried to explain to her that this was army life, if an emergency happened somewhere in the world, he could suddenly be gone for months. It had all come to a head when it was announced that the Regiment was being posted to Berlin for two years, in a few months' time. Of course, wives could accompany their husbands and live in the Married Quarters, but Stinky knew there was no way Brenda would leave Dudley. She had her family and old friends living close by, and unlike Stinky, had no desire to see the rest of the world. She was so happy when he told her that he was leaving the army, that she didn't even raise any objections when he'd told her that he and Dennis intended on becoming Private Investigators.

A Few Weeks Later

The paperwork had all been done. Not surprisingly, Buckethead had asked Stinky to reconsider.

"One day, obviously, many years from now, you could have my job. Planet Plunkett could be all yours," he'd said.

Dennis had almost pointed out that in that case, it would be Planet Blackshaw but had felt it best to keep quiet. The Colour Sergeant had tried everything but soon realised that Stinky's mind was made up. Eventually, he had said, "Fair enough, lad, I think you'll regret it, but good luck for the future." Then he'd turned to look at Dennis. Dennis had been amazed thinking his old adversary was about also to wish him good luck, but after staring at him for a few seconds, Buckethead suddenly screamed, "Get down Bisskit and give me twenty." As Dennis completed his last push-up, he heard Buckethead say, "I'm going to miss seeing you do that, Bisskit," and then the door slammed behind him.

The big day got closer, and the lads knew there was no leaving the army behind without a huge going away booze-up. Their friends kept coming up with different ideas until it was eventually decided that a fancy-dress party was the way to go. This would basically involve a huge pub-crawl around Lichfield, wearing some form of fancy dress. The lads had been involved in enough of these events to know that the chances of them surviving the evening without some sort of disaster occurring were slim, especially when Dennis Bisskit was involved.

"So, what do you think?" Stinky asked as he paraded in front of his friend.

Dennis looked him up and down. Stinky was wearing a long wig, a bright red headband, a flowery shirt and bell-bottomed jeans.

"I don't get it, what are you supposed to be?"

Stinky held up two fingers in a V sign and said, "Peace man, I'm a hippie, Ginge."

Dennis nodded and said, "It will have to do, Stinky, but my advice to you is, do not let Buckethead see you wearing that outfit. You could well be responsible for him having a heart attack."

Stinky had another look at his reflection in the mirror.

"Well, I think I look great. Come on then, Ginge, you know you're dying to show me your outfit."

Dennis disappeared behind his metal bedside locker and a few minutes later reappeared. He was wearing a large pirate's hat, a long, black beard and a frilly, red shirt. In one hand, he held a plastic cutlass, and on his other hand, he had attached a plastic hook. On his shoulder was a toy budgerigar.

Stinky stared for so long that eventually, Dennis said,

"Admit it, it's great."

"Are you really going to walk around town with a budgerigar on your shoulder?" Stinky asked.

Dennis shrugged. "It's not ideal, but parrots are very difficult to find. Anyway, if anyone asks, I'll just say I'm working my way up. It was going cheap at the pet shop. Do you get it, a budgerigar going cheap?"

Stinky looked confused, so Dennis continued, "They even threw this in, for free."

He held up a large black flag with a white skull and crossbones, embroidered upon it. Then, he suddenly looked serious and added,

"You know we will have to be very alert tonight. We need to keep our wits about us, or else the entire evening could end in disaster."

Stinky looked confused again, so Dennis enlightened him.

"You remember what happened to Stumpy Gibbons last year when he left the Regiment?"

Stinky shook his head.

"He was found the next morning, in the centre of Lichfield. Tied naked to a lamppost and covered in strawberry jam. Not only that, but they had tied a couple of pork sausages around his waist. I saw Stumpy the next morning; he was still traumatised. He told me it took three people to drag that German Shepherd off him."

Stinky laughed.

"Our friends wouldn't do that. It's just going to be a nice, quiet evening of reminiscing over a couple of drinks."

Dennis shook his head.

"You may be right my friend, but I'm taking no chances. The first sign of strawberry jam and I'm off."

At six pm, the lads piled onto the minibus. Corporal Jimmy 'Big Ears' Jackson, from the Transport Section, had agreed, for a small fee, to borrow the bus and drive them into Lichfield. He would also return at closing time to pick them up. The minibus wasn't actually his to use, and so he'd emphasised that they must be on their best behaviour, keep the noise down and keep a low profile. They had instantly agreed, and he had foolishly believed them.

Fifteen lads, in various forms of fancy dress, piled aboard, and before the bus had even left the barracks, Big Ears realised that he might have made a mistake. The lads had started the festivities in the NAAFI bar a couple of hours earlier and were already in a jovial mood. They immediately started opening bottles of beer, even though Big Ears pointed out that it would only take a few minutes to reach their destination. To calm them down, he turned his tape recorder on and turned the volume up. Next time he glanced in the rear-view mirror, the lads were all singing along to *Hey Jude,* whilst Dennis and Stinky danced in the aisle.

He sighed with relief as he watched the lads disappear into the Swan Hotel. Thankfully, they were now someone else's problem. At least until closing time.

It was turning into a great evening of drinking, laughter, singing and reminiscing about the last few years. They had started off in the Swan Hotel, then moved on to the Bowling Green, then the Cross Keys, then the King's Head and now had finally landed in The Chequer's. Dennis took a swig from his pint of Ansell's Light Ale, turned to Stinky and slurred, "I cujent 'ave manished without you my old matee!!!" Stinky laughed. His friend had never been much of a drinker, although he was making a big effort tonight. Every now and again he would run around the bar, holding his pirate's flag above his head and shouting, "Ahoy, me mateys, another drink for Captain Dennis."

"Never mind, Ginge," Stinky told him, "I got you through the army, and now you can get me through being a Private Investigator." Dennis nodded and was just about to tell Stinky about some of his ideas for their new business venture when he was overcome with an urgent need to visit the toilet. His friend laughed again as Dennis staggered across the room. Amazingly, his pirate's outfit was still in one piece, although the blue and white striped pyjama bottoms that he'd worn for some reason were now looking a bit tattered, as was the skull and crossbones flag draped around his shoulders.

Dennis sat on the toilet, suddenly feeling slightly sick. He heard laughter and shouting as others entered the room but paid little attention until he heard the words "strawberry jam" mentioned. Whoever was talking: obviously did not realise Dennis was in one of the cubicles. He listened intently as they discussed their plans.

His first thought was to warn Stinky, but when he looked around the bar, his friend was nowhere to be seen. Making sure no one was watching him, he picked up a large bottle of pale ale someone had bought him, carefully backed out of the bar and staggered outside. He searched all around the pub, but there was no sign of his friend. Eventually, Dennis convinced himself that Stinky must have either met a girl or returned to camp for some reason. He stood by the side of the road that would take him back to the barracks, stuck his thumb in the air, and a few moments later, miraculously, a car stopped to give him a lift, he climbed in and instantly fell asleep.

Next thing he knew he was being woken up by someone he didn't recognise and trying to recall how he got there. The stranger shook him again and shouted, "Come on, you're at Whittington Barracks, go and get a good night's sleep."

Dennis suddenly remembered, he had got a lift back to camp. With some difficulty, he managed to extract himself from the car, shouted, "Thank you muchly," and was amazed to see that he still held the open bottle of beer in his hand. "Nishly done Dennish," he slurred to himself, "never spilt a drop." He walked through the camp entrance and passed the small guard room. "Ahoy, me mateys," he shouted and was met by a torrent of abuse from someone inside.

He took a swig from the bottle and continued towards his accommodation block, across the large parade square, where nearly six years earlier he had first arrived with Stinky and met Buckethead. He chuckled to himself just thinking about it. Then he heard a sound from above, glancing up he realised he was standing beneath the flagpole. High above him, the flag of the Staffordshire Regiment fluttered in the breeze.

The idea came to him in a flash, a way to leave his mark, it was brilliant. Years from now, blokes would say, "Remember what Bisskit did just before he left? He's a legend."

He untied the rope from around the hook and tried to lower the regimental flag, but after trying for a few minutes, he realised that for some reason it was stuck. He then decided that if the flag wasn't going to come down to him, he would have to go up and get it. He placed the large bottle of beer on the ground, made sure the pirate's flag was secure around his shoulders and grasped the flagpole.

Discussing it days later with Stinky, they had both agreed that had he been sober, there was no way he could have climbed it, but having drunk enough to remove all fear of heights, he eventually found himself clinging to the top of the wooden pole, staring at the flag. With great difficulty, he managed to unclip the regimental flag, drop it to the ground and replace it with the skull and crossbones. He was so impressed that he very nearly stepped back to admire his handiwork, but then realised where he was.

At that precise moment, two things happened. Firstly, he instantly sobered up, and secondly, he suddenly heard shouting and cheering. The flagpole was starting to sway around in the breeze. He wrapped his arms and legs tightly around it and glanced down towards the parade square, he could see a crowd had gathered. The lads must have arrived back from town and were cheering him on.

"Well done, Captain Dennis."

"Brilliant, Ginge."

"Ahoy, Captain."

And then a new voice echoed across the square.

"Get down off that flagpole, Bisskit, you horrible man."

Dennis looked in the direction of the voice and through the gloom saw Buckethead striding towards him. He was so shocked that for a moment he relaxed his feet and instantly felt himself sliding rapidly down the flagpole. He tried to slow down but could not get a grip with his legs and just slid faster and faster until suddenly, he hit the concrete ground. Unable to stop himself, his legs buckled, and he sat down. A scream rang through the night.

Dennis slowly stood up on shaking legs. There was a loud gasp from the watching crowd; even Buckethead seemed stunned. Dennis just stood there for a few seconds with the large beer bottle stuck into his right buttock. Then it fell to the ground and smashed; blood started to trickle down Dennis's tattered, blue and white striped pyjamas.

"Shiver me timbers, lads, I am wounded," he groaned, before fainting to the ground.

The following morning, Stinky stared down at his friend. Dennis was lying on his stomach on a hospital bed.

"Oh, good of you to pop in, Stinky," he moaned, "and where have you been all night whilst I was at death's door?"

"Sorry, Ginge, I only woke up a couple of hours ago, naked in the main street."

Dennis sighed.

"I warned you. Strawberry jam?"

Stinky nodded.

"Pork sausages?"

"Just a couple," Stinky replied, "Luckily, there were no dogs about. Anyway, I missed out on all the fun. You are the talk of the regiment, Ginge; you're a legend."

Dennis nodded, he didn't feel very legendary at that point in time.

Stinky stared at the towel covering his friend's back and eventually said,

"Can I have a look?"

Dennis thought long and hard and then replied.

"One quick look and then it must never be mentioned again."

Stinky carefully pulled the towel back and stared at the circle of stitches in the middle of Dennis's right buttock.

"Wow, it's uncanny," he gasped, "it's exactly the same wound as your dad. You will have a scar just like him."

Dennis tried to manoeuvre himself into a more comfortable position and then said,

"Well, I suppose that's one good thing. Much better to have the scar there, out of the way, than in the middle of my forehead."

Part 2

Chapter 13
March 1969

The following morning, when Dennis met Stinky outside his house, he was looking unusually smart, in a blue, pin-striped suit and red tie. Stinky stared at him and asked, "Are you off to help your dad at a funeral because I thought we were busy."

Dennis did a fake chuckle and said, "Oh, very amusing, Stinky, very droll. No, it's just that I felt that now we are working on a major M.P. Case, that's Missing Person, by the way. I felt it was time we started to look a bit more professional; I think if we want people to take us seriously, we need to start looking like proper Private Investigators." With that, he reached into his jacket pocket and pulled out a couple of cards; he handed one to Stinky who stared at it for a moment and then said, "It's a piece of card you've cut out of a Cornflakes' packet." Dennis quickly reached across and turned the card over so that his friend could read it.

'JACK BLACKSHAW, PRIVATE INVESTIGATOR'.

And then underneath in smaller writing, a contact number. "It's just temporary until we get proper ones made, I put Jack instead of Stinky because that looks more professional as well."

Stinky put the card in his pocket and said, "Good, Brenda will be pleased, she hates it when people call me Stinky, and tomorrow I will wear my one and only suit. I, too, can look professional, in fact, I would say I will probably look even more professional than you because I won't have a large slice of cake stuck to my shoulder." Dennis twisted his head down, groaned and wiped the lump of stale cake off the shoulder of his suit.

"I wondered why people were staring at me," he mumbled, "I assumed it was because I looked so smart."

Stinky laughed and said, "Don't worry, my old friend, nothing says I'm a professional like a slice of cake attached to your shoulder."

They sat in their office drinking tea and decided on a plan of action. Buckethead had given them the address of the house he had been renting. He had also given them the key. He was living in the camp at Whittington Barracks, but the rent was paid up for another week, and he hadn't got around to handing the key in. He had told them that the house was empty, and he had already checked for any clues Gloria may have left behind, but Dennis had said, "I'm sure you did your best, but we are highly trained in this sort of thing." Buckethead had given him the sort of look that was usually followed by, "Get down you horrible man and give me twenty," but instead he'd eventually said, "Fair enough, whatever you think is best."

They followed the written directions to an area near Lichfield they had rarely passed through. "I can't understand why Buckethead would pay good money to rent a house all the way out here when he could live in the Married Quarters on the camp for next to nothing," Stinky said.

"Soldiers," Dennis explained. "I remember Gloria telling me that he hated her going anywhere near any soldiers. So, he kept her as far away as possible."

Stinky glanced over at him. "Have you never seen Gloria since that day at her house in Dover?"

Dennis kept looking ahead but eventually said, "No way. She was great, but Buckethead would have killed me if I'd gone anywhere near her. Anyway, I don't think she would have wanted to see me again after I pretended to be an actor."

Stinky smiled. "See, I told you to pretend you were a doctor; even Buckethead would have been happy if his daughter was going out with a pretend doctor."

Dennis pulled up outside of a plain looking house. Even from the outside, it looked unlived in. As they walked down the path, Dennis glanced over at the house next door and saw a curtain move. They used the key Buckethead had given them, opened the front door and entered the house. Stinky shouted "Hello" just in case, but his greeting just echoed around the empty house. Their footsteps sounded very loud as they walked from room to room. They checked through the downstairs rooms first, but there was very little to see, just some basic furniture, table, chairs, a sofa. They moved the sofa and checked underneath it and then felt down the sides of the cushions. Stinky suddenly smiled, held his hand up and shouted, "A shilling."

"That makes it all worthwhile then," Dennis muttered and then added, "I think we may be wasting our time here, mate. I'll tell you what, you check upstairs, and I'll pop next door and see if…" he checked the piece of paper Buckethead had given them. "Beverly is in; evidently, she and Gloria are quite close."

He strode around to the neighbour's house, knocked on the front door and waited. Then knocked again, louder. Dennis thought he heard movement, so he opened the letterbox and shouted, "Hello, is Beverly there?" He noticed some pink roses growing next to the door and leaned forward to smell one of the blooms.

Suddenly, the door opened, and a young woman with dirty blonde hair stuck her head out. "What do you want, I'm trying to get some sleep, I work in the evening." She was amazed to see a short, ginger-haired man, rolling around on the garden path, holding his nose. He suddenly leapt to his feet, screaming, and punched himself in the face. Then, whilst the woman looked on in amazement, he placed a thumb on his left nostril and blew with all his might. All manner of things shot out of his right nostril. Dennis took a couple of deep breaths, flattened his wayward ginger hair down a bit and held out his right hand.

"Bumblebee up the nose," he muttered as if that explained everything. She didn't seem to be interested in shaking his hand, so instead, he showed her his card, "I'm sorry to disturb you, I just wanted to ask you a few questions about Gloria from next door."

She stared at the card and finally said, "This is just a piece of a Cornflakes' packet."

Dennis quickly reached across and turned the card over. "Sorry, that's just temporary, my proper card is in the post."

She glanced at it and handed it back. "I'm afraid I can't help you, I've been away for a couple of weeks on holiday. Only got back this morning, they had all left."

"Did Gloria tell you where she might be going?" Dennis asked.

She shrugged her shoulders. "As I say, when I got back they had gone, so I didn't get a chance to talk to her." Dennis had a feeling she wasn't telling the truth. Buckethead had told them that Gloria and Beverly were good friends, surely, they would have discussed Gloria's plans.

"Look, Beverly," Dennis said, "Gloria is not in any trouble. She is a grown woman; she can do what she wants. The only thing is her mother and father are terribly upset; they just want to know that she is safe. In fact, her father should be in Germany by now, but he's had to get leave so he can search for her."

Beverly nodded. "I know, I saw him Wednesday, looking around the house, but as I say, I can't help you, I have to get some sleep." With that, she turned and slammed the door.

As he closed the front gate, he nearly bumped into Stinky, who started to say something, but Dennis muttered, "In a minute. Let's get out of sight first." They jumped into the car and drove down the road and around the corner before Dennis pulled over to the kerb.

"Beverly knows something, I could tell by her manner, and then she lied. First, she told me she had been away for two weeks and only got back this morning, and then she told me that she had seen Buckethead next door, last Wednesday."

Stinky thought about what this meant, and then suddenly remembered his news. "I searched the bathroom, and behind the waste-bin by the side of the bath, I found this," he held up a necklace. "Looks like someone took it off to have a bath and it fell behind the bin. It could be Gloria's or her mother's."

Dennis held it up to the light; it was a gold chain with a cross attached to it. "It's Gloria's," he told his friend. "She showed it to me the first night we met. Her grandmother left it to her. She said she wore it all the time."

Dennis suddenly had a plan. He explained it to Stinky. He turned the car around and drove back to where they had just come from. As he opened the front gate to Beverley's house, they nearly bumped into one another. Dennis apologised, "Sorry, I was hoping to catch you before you went back to sleep."

Beverly looked flustered and eventually said, "I was just checking to see if there was any post. What do you want now?"

Dennis held up the gold necklace. "Look, we found this, I know it belongs to Gloria, but we can't waste any more time looking for her. I was just thinking, could you look after it, because she may well come back looking for it. I know it meant a lot to her."

Beverly looked undecided for a moment but then took the necklace. "Okay, I doubt if she will come back, but if I see her, I will give it to her." Dennis made a gesture with his hands as if to indicate he wasn't really concerned one way or another and walked off saying, "Sorry to bother you."

As he walked to the car, he could feel her eyes watching him. He drove back down the street and around the corner, but this time carried on in a big circle until he approached Beverley's house from the opposite direction. He pulled in behind a van parked about thirty yards from her house and ate the cheese and onion sandwich which Stinky offered him. After about ten minutes, they saw the front gate open, and Beverly emerged. She quickly looked up and down the street, and then, seemingly satisfied that no one was watching, she strode off down the road. Dennis pulled out from behind the van, and keeping a good distance away from her, he slowly followed. "She could be going anywhere," Stinky said, but then she stepped into a bus shelter and sat down. Dennis pulled over to the kerb. The lads waited a moment, and then Stinky reached into the glove compartment and pulled out a handful of coins. "I hope she's not going abroad; I told Brenda I'd be home for tea." He stepped out of the car, wrapped a scarf around his neck, pulled a woollen cap down almost to his eyes, told Dennis he'd call him when he had news and made his way to the bus stop.

Dennis waited in the office for a few hours then went home and was just settling down to beans on toast, when the phone went. "I'm worn out; she went all the way into the city," Stinky sounded in a bad mood.

"What, Lichfield?" Dennis asked.

"No, the big city, Birmingham. I lost her in the crowd for a moment, and then I spotted her entering the Midland Hotel, you know, that old fancy place on New Street." Dennis nodded as if his friend could see him, and maybe he could because he continued. "She was nowhere to be seen, so I waited in the foyer, and after about half an hour, she came down the stairs that lead to the guest rooms. She was looking around, Ginge, as if she feared being followed. She went out and got straight on a bus heading home, closely followed by me."

Dennis was quiet for a moment and then mumbled, "I wonder if she was meeting Gloria, she might be staying at the hotel."

Stinky had saved his big news for last. "I think she was, Ginge, because all the way there she held Gloria's necklace in her hand, she kept twisting it around her fingers like she was nervous. On the journey back, it had disappeared."

Chapter 14

They stood near the entrance to the Midland Hotel, waiting for the right moment. An elderly couple came through the large glass doors, and they watched as the doorman rushed forward to help put their bags into a taxi. Stinky glanced into the foyer. "Okay, it looks quiet enough now."

Dennis didn't look happy. "How come I have to make the distraction?" he asked.

Stinky smiled, "You've spent your life making distractions, it just comes naturally to you." Before his friend could argue anymore, Stinky strode through the glass doors and walked purposefully towards the reception desk. When he was halfway there, he glanced back over his shoulder and saw a remarkable thing. Dennis, who had entered the hotel a few seconds behind him, suddenly let out a groan, threw himself backwards on to the carpeted floor and began jerking his arms and legs in all directions. Stinky was so fascinated that he almost forgot what he was doing, but as he turned back, he was pleased to see the white-faced receptionist leaving her desk and racing towards Dennis, shouting for help as she ran. Stinky ignored the noise and stepped behind the desk. He quickly found the Guest Registration Book but could see no sign of a Gloria Plunkett signing in over the last few days. He heard more shouting and realised it was Dennis, who was now throwing himself around so violently, that he was practically levitating. Just as Stinky was about to give up, he noticed a sign taped to the desk with some names on it. He ran back towards his friend shouting, "What's wrong, is he okay?"

The receptionist, with the help of a couple of guests, was trying to hold Dennis down, but as soon as he heard Stinky's shout, he stopped shaking, sat up and said, "Yes, I'm fine now, just one of my old turns." By now the manager had arrived and tried to get Dennis to sit down whilst they called for an ambulance, but he insisted that all he needed was a cup of tea, so eventually they left him to it. The manager seemingly happy to avoid the attention an ambulance at the front door might cause. To one side of the foyer were some tables and chairs. They found a good spot where they could keep an eye on the place and ordered a pot of tea.

"Well, I must say, that was a superb performance," Stinky told his friend.

Dennis shrugged his shoulders as if it were nothing. "Remember, I had a lot of practice when I met Gloria I was pretending to be one of the finest actors in Dudley."

Stinky laughed and said, "Dudley!! Come on now, young Bisskit, there's no need for false modesty. You are easily the finest pretend actor in the entire West Midlands."

A lady wearing a white blouse with MIDLAND HOTEL printed on the chest brought them their pot of tea and asked Dennis if he was feeling okay now. "Fine," he told her, "it's an old war wound, but life has to go on."

She patted him on the shoulder and said, "I'll bring you some biscuits, on the house."

Stinky nodded his head in appreciation. "No one lies as good as you Ginge; it's a gift." Dennis looked quite proud but then asked his friend if he'd found anything in the Guest Book. Stinky told him that he hadn't but had spotted a name on the Staff List, a Gloria Jackson, Room 114. Dennis was confused until Stinky explained, "Remember the house we searched this morning in Jackson Road? I'm thinking she may have got a job here and changed her name, in case anyone came looking, maybe Jackson was the first name that came into her head." The waitress brought a plate of custard creams, and they dunked them in their tea as they looked out for Gloria.

Ten minutes later, Dennis suddenly slammed his cup of tea down onto the table, picked up the menu and held it in front of his face. Stinky turned around in his seat just in time to see the back of a young woman running up the staircase. Dennis peeped over the top of the menu to check the coast was clear and said, "It's her."

Stinky stood up, but his friend hesitated and then said, "Do you mind if I meet her on my own first, I would like to try and explain things to her." Stinky understood, he nodded and sat back down.

Dennis walked up to the fifth floor, following the directions, and walked along the corridor until he reached Room 114. He stood there for several minutes trying to work out what he would say and then eventually tapped on the door. After some moments' silence, the door opened, and Gloria stood in front of him. Her hair was longer than the last time he had seen her, she was wearing the hotel uniform of white blouse and black skirt and looked more beautiful than ever. She looked at him for a moment and then gasped, "Dennis Bisskit, what are you doing here, how did you find me?"

Dennis finally found his voice, smiled and told her, "I'm a Private Investigator, that's what I do."

She turned and slammed the door in his face, but before he could even move, she opened the door again. She didn't look happy. "So, is this a movie role you are playing, or are you playing a soldier pretending to be a Private Investigator, I get confused."

Dennis knew he had to explain quickly before she slammed the door again. "I really am a Private Investigator," he told her, handing her his card.

She shook her head. "What's this, a piece of a Cornflakes packet?"

He quickly turned it over so she could read the other side. "Look, Gloria, please let me explain. That night when I met you in Dover, I knew you didn't like soldiers and I really wanted to talk to you, so I pretended to be an actor. It just got out of hand. I was going to confess at your house, but then suddenly your dad appeared, and that was it, after that, I didn't get a chance."

She stared at him for a while and then said, "Well, it certainly explained why you knew so little about Shakespeare." Then she started laughing, "You must have had a heart attack when you found out who my father was."

Dennis nodded. "I still sometimes have nightmares about it. I wasn't his favourite soldier before, and that just made things worse."

She was still smiling, which Dennis felt was a good sign. "I've never seen him so angry with me; he told me that I must

65

never speak to you again and that you were the worst soldier in the Regiment."

Dennis looked offended and said, "That's ridiculous, there were at least two soldiers as bad as me. Anyway, Gloria, it's great to see you again, you look wonderful."

She frowned. "Thank you, but you still haven't explained what you are doing here," Dennis told her his business partner was waiting in the foyer, and they could explain there over a cup of tea. She looked at her watch and grabbed her room key. "Okay, I was just going to get some lunch."

"So, you two left the army and became Private Investigators?" Gloria said between sips of tea, "I didn't even know that was a real job."

Stinky offered her a biscuit and told her, "Well, to be honest, looking for you is the biggest job we have had so far."

She slammed her cup down onto the table and turned to Dennis. "You were looking for me? I thought it was just a coincidence that you came into the hotel."

Dennis tried to find the right words, "Gloria, you just disappeared, your mum and dad are so worried, your dad should be in Germany, but he took leave to look for you, then he came to see us and hired us to find you."

Gloria couldn't believe it; she just stared at the table for a minute. "I didn't think he would be bothered. As usual, he just assumed that I would want to go to Germany for two years. I'm nearly twenty-one, I'm sick of travelling and not knowing anybody. Mum doesn't seem to mind, she thinks it's her duty, but I want my own life. A friend of mine worked as a chambermaid here and was leaving, she told me about it, and the best was, I get my own room."

"Was that friend Beverly?" Stinky asked. Gloria looked surprised. So he explained, "We are Private Investigators, that's what we do."

She suddenly understood, "You followed Beverly here, that's how you found me," and then asked, "Does Dad know yet?"

Dennis shook his head. "Not yet, we wanted to be sure, but you really need to see him, Gloria. He has been so worried; I think he will understand."

Gloria told them she was going to write a letter that evening anyway and send it to the camp in Germany, explaining everything and assuring her parents that she was safe and sound. "I love working here and just talking to people," she told them. "It's a lovely place; it has a lot of history to it. Do you know we pump water up from a well beneath the hotel? There are old tunnels down there that go for miles underneath the city centre."

"Sounds interesting," Dennis told her, "I used to be a bellboy at The Victoria Hotel in Wolverhampton, you know."

She chuckled. "You are just full of surprises, Dennis Bisskit, bellboy, actor, soldier, investigator. Is there anything else I should know?"

Before he could answer, Stinky said, "Believe me, Gloria, there are some things in life you are better off not knowing."

Chapter 15

Buckethead had been unusually quiet when Dennis had rung him and told him that they had found Gloria, and she would meet him in their office. Now he sat looking uncomfortable and strangely nervous. "I've always tried to be a good father and protect her," he told them, "but there are a lot of bad people out there, especially when you leave the safety of Planet Plunkett."

As he said this, he stared at Dennis until eventually Dennis felt compelled to say, "You do know, Sir, I'm actually not a bad person." Before Buckethead could reply, there was a nervous tap on the door. Dennis opened it slightly, mumbled a few words and then turned and motioned to Stinky. They stepped out of the office, and Gloria stepped in.

There were no raised voices, in fact, it was so quiet that Dennis started to get a bit concerned, but after about fifteen minutes, the office door suddenly opened, and Gloria and her father came out into the corridor. Buckethead handed Dennis an envelope. "Money well spent," he said. "I underestimated you lads. Thank you for finding my daughter. It would appear that she is now grown up and ready to leave the safety of Planet Plunkett." Father and daughter hugged, and then without a word he started to walk away. Then, he suddenly stopped and turned back to Dennis. "Since I will be serving my country in Germany, I am holding you personally responsible for my daughter's welfare, Mr Bisskit, and if so much as a hair on her head comes to any harm, you will be doing push-ups until you are an extremely old man. Do we have an understanding?"

Dennis nodded.

Chapter 16
A Week Later

Dennis dropped the newspaper onto the office table. Stinky looked up. "What's wrong with you?" he asked. Dennis shook his head, "I can't believe it, I just cannot believe it. The Man from Paris with the Very Large Head has gone."

Stinky looked confused, "What man from Paris? Gone where?"

Dennis explained as if he were talking to a child, "The Man from Paris with the Very Large Head has been stolen. It's by Picasso. It's a tragedy, Stinky."

Stinky didn't seem impressed. "So, I presume this is a painting of some French chap with a head completely out of proportion with the rest of his body, why should we be worried?"

Dennis tutted and shook his head from side to side. "Oh, my dear Stinky, I despair sometimes, you really do know absolutely nothing about art. This painting is priceless. Interestingly, it was the last one he did during his Frenchmen with Large Heads period, immediately after this, he moved on to his Spanish Women with Unusual Noses' period. Police say it's a total mystery. It was hanging on the wall of the Birmingham Art Gallery and Museum when they locked up, and the next morning it was gone. It's a shame because I was going to invite Gloria to visit the exhibition with me this weekend."

Stinky smirked. "Oh I see, and no doubt you were going to impress her with your vast knowledge of Picasso, which you, in fact, got from last Sunday's newspaper, I know because I read the same article. Believe it or not, I don't just read the Sports Section. Strange that you are now a fan, because I distinctly remember that when we were at school, we went on a visit to the Art Gallery and you saw a painting of a woman by Picasso, and you said it was the biggest load of rubbish you had ever seen. In fact, your exact words were, 'He can't even get her nose in the correct position; I wouldn't pay him to paint Granddad's shed.'"

Dennis thought about denying ever saying that but instead said, "Well, I was very young then, Stinky, but over the years I have come to appreciate his style. Anyway, I think we should visit the Art Gallery and check it out."

"Why?" Stinky asked, "The police will be on to it, what can we do?"

Dennis looked at the article in the newspaper again and then said, "Two very good reasons. One, the gallery is offering a 5,000-pound reward, and two, we would bring a certain something to the case that the police would not." He stared into space trying to think what that certain something was.

Stinky tried to help him.

"Incompetence?"

"No."

"Amateurishness?"

"No, and I don't think that's a real word."

"A total lack of knowledge of the subject?"

"No." Dennis looked back at his friend and said, "I'm not sure what we will bring, Stinky, but the main thing is, we will bring it, don't worry about that."

The lads drove into the city and made their way slowly towards The Birmingham Art Gallery and Museum. "I hate driving in the city," Dennis moaned, "there are just people everywhere."

Stinky nodded. "I suppose that's why it's called a city though, if there were no people around, it would be more of a village with a lot of buildings in it," he ventured.

They parked as close as they could and walked up to the impressive looking building. A large clock tower, known locally as 'Big Brum' cast a shadow over them. They walked up the concrete steps and entered through the big glass doors. The first person they spotted was the newly promoted Detective Sergeant Pratt, an old friend of Dennis's father. "Hello, Dennis, Stinky," he shouted, "not seen you lads for a while, are you still getting paid by suspicious husbands to follow their wives?" The last time Dennis had seen him, he had been quite dismissive about Dennis's new career, saying, "That sort of thing might work for the Yanks, but over here we have real policemen to do police work." Dennis said hello and then asked DS Pratt about the robbery. He smiled and said, "Now don't get poking your nose into important crimes like that boys. All I'm at liberty to say is this, I have some leads and expect to make an early arrest." As he said this, he stared to his front, as if he were speaking into a television camera.

"You don't mind if we have a look around?" Dennis asked. "Well, the Art Gallery is open to the public," DS Pratt replied, "and you are members of the public. Just keep out of the way of the professionals." With that, he turned and strode off as if he had more important things to do.

The Art Gallery and Museum actually consisted of many galleries and exhibits; you could easily get lost in there. So, Dennis picked up a leaflet showing a layout of the building, and they walked into the small café near the building entrance to grab a cuppa and work out exactly where they were. As Dennis waited for Stinky to come back with their pot of tea, he noticed a tired looking cleaning lady walk past carrying a mop and bucket. He found a free table and studied the leaflet until he found the Picasso Exhibition room.

Later, when they tried to check the room out, they found it was 'Temporarily Closed', and a uniformed policeman was standing guard outside. "We may as well come back tomorrow, when the excitement has died down a bit," Stinky suggested. Dennis agreed. As they walked out, they passed a surly looking man in a dark suit. He had short, grey hair, and on his suit jacket was a shiny badge with SECURITY' written on it. As they left the building, Stinky chuckled and said, "No wonder he looks unhappy, he has to explain how The Man from Paris with the Very Large Head has gone missing on his watch."

Dennis nodded and replied, "Yes, it can't help his career. Personally, I was more interested in the other badge, the small one on his lapel."

The lads were back sitting in their parked car.

"Are you sure?" Stinky asked. Dennis looked offended.

"Of course, I'm sure, have you ever known me to make a mistake?"

"Well…"

But before Stinky could commence with his long list, Dennis continued,

"He is definitely wearing a Staffordshire Regimental Badge. The knot, the crown, the feathers. I saw it because that's what I do, Stinky, I observe things. That's why people call me The Great Observer of Dudley."

Stinky looked surprised. "I didn't know that. You've told me that you'd been called The Sherlock Holmes of Dudley and The Fred Astaire of Dudley and The Sir Lawrence Olivier of Dudley. Plus, I know for a fact that you have been called lots and lots of less complimentary names, but I must say I did not realise that you were also known as The Great Observer of Dudley."

Dennis was busy staring at his reflection in the rearview mirror and adjusting his hair but stopped long enough to say, "Well, that's why you are not known as The Great Observer of Dudley, Stinky, because you are not as observant as I am. Anyway, the point is, us all being ex- Staffies, he may tell us things that he didn't tell the police, but before we talk to him, I want to call in a favour from Buckethead, see if he knows anything that might help."

As soon as they got back to the office, Dennis found the phone number in his little book and dialled Whittington Barracks. Whilst he waited, he said, "I hope he hasn't already left for Berlin," then he heard a voice on the other end of the phone. Stinky listened to the conversation.

"Yes, hello, I'd like to speak to Warrant Officer Plunkett, please…

I don't care how busy he is; it's very important…

You will be in even more trouble if he doesn't get this call, just mention my name, Dennis Bisskit."

Dennis smiled at Stinky, "That's sorted him out, he's gone to fetch him."

Suddenly, Dennis pulled the phone away from his ear; Stinky could hear shouting and screaming coming through the speaker.

"It's me, Sir, Dennis, Dennis Bisskit…

But you said to call if I ever had a problem…

Well, how was I to know you were only joking?"

The conversation went on for several minutes, with Dennis writing down the odd bit of information and occasionally nodding his head in agreement as if Buckethead could see it.

Eventually, Dennis said, "Well, thank you, Sir, and good luck in… Oh …he's put the phone down."

He looked up and said, "Good news and bad news. He knows the security man at the Art Gallery; his name is Charles Dawkins, he left the Regiment not long before we joined in '63. The bad news is that it's no good, us saying Buckethead sent us. Evidently, he hates him. They were both sergeants, and Dawkins thought he should have got the promotion to Colour Sergeant, but Plunkett got it instead."

"Lucky for us really," Stinky said, "he looked even grumpier than Buckethead, it's hard to imagine, but things could have been even worse." Then he added, "So, he couldn't help then?"

"Well, he did give me one thing, he said the best way to get in with Dawkins is to talk cricket; evidently, he's mad about it, he goes to every game at…" Dennis consulted his notes. "Hedge… Something."

"Edgbaston," Stinky said helpfully. "The home of Warwickshire Cricket Club and M.J.K. Smith, England's finest player."

"That's probably the place."

"Well, I better talk to him, because you know absolutely nothing about cricket," Stinky said, and then added, "unless, of course, you are The Great Cricketer of Dudley and haven't told me about it."

But Dennis ignored the sarcasm; he had other ideas. "No, don't worry, I'll sort that out, I have a better job for a man of your good looks and charm."

"I hate it when you compliment me," Stinky muttered, "it's normally followed by something bad."

"I don't know what you're talking about," Dennis said, looking aggrieved.

"When we were in the café, I noticed a cleaning lady; someone called her Jean. After lunch, you should talk to her. Cleaning ladies are like hairdressers; they know everything that's going on. Just use the old Blackshaw charm and find out what you can, anything unusual she may have heard or noticed. Meanwhile, I'm going to pop around and see my granddad, I've had a bit of an idea."

Chapter 17

Dennis had almost given up searching, when suddenly, there it was lying on a shelf in the shed. An old cricket bat.

He had recalled his granddad throwing it in the shed some time back. The thought had occurred to him, that if he walked past Mr Dawkins carrying a cricket bat, he was bound to be impressed. He took it out into the sunshine and dusted it down with his hand. Suddenly, he spotted a signature written near the handle: J. Smith. *No, surely it can't be*, he thought and raced into the house to speak to his grandfather.

He had assumed that his granddad would be happy to see the back of an old cricket bat that he had thrown into the shed, but he immediately grabbed it off Dennis and held it close to his chest, like he was hugging a baby. "Careful with that, it's priceless," he told his grandson, then he turned it over and said, "see that signature, it's a J. Smith."

"Yes, I see it," Dennis said, "would that be the great England player, M.J.K. Smith?"

"It could be."

"Yes, but is it?"

Granddad hesitated and then explained, "It's Jemima Smith, I've known her for years at the Bingo. I took my old bat in once and got her to sign it for a joke. I thought J. Smith would look good on it."

"Has she ever actually played cricket?" Dennis asked.

"I very much doubt it; she works in Grimshaw's factory, making safety pins."

"Is she any relation to M.J.K. Smith?" Dennis inquired hopefully.

Granddad thought for a moment and then smiled and said, "Her aunt lived in the same street as the cricketer's mother, so she may be distantly related."

It was time for the negotiations to begin, so Dennis got straight to the point.

"Okay, so what we actually have here is just an old cricket bat, with the signature of a lady who makes safety pins scribbled on it. So, when you say it is priceless, what does that actually mean?"

After some hard-negotiating, Dennis managed to get it down to two bottles of brown ale and left the house with the bat tucked under his arm wrapped up in an old potato sack. He drove around to Stinky's house to pick him up, and they sat in the car for a while to discuss their plans.

"How will I find this cleaning lady?" Stinky asked.

"You can't miss her, she looks just like that young actress you like," Dennis told him, "Jane somebody." Stinky looked baffled, so Dennis added, "You know, she was in that film about hairdressers."

Stinky suddenly realised who it was his friend was talking about. "Do you mean Jane Fonda?" Dennis nodded. Stinky shook his head. "You do realise Barbarella has nothing whatsoever to do with a barber's shop." They drove to the Art Gallery, split up and agreed to meet in the café in thirty minutes.

Dennis immediately spotted the security guard; he was standing outside a small office, studying a notepad and looking at least as grumpy as he had the first time they had seen him. Dennis tucked the sack containing the cricket bat under his arm and casually walked past him. As he passed, Dennis glanced up, leapt backwards as if he'd seen a ghost and said. "No, it can't be, surely not. I don't believe it, aren't you Charles Dawkins, the former legend of the Staffordshire Regiment?"

The man looked him up and down and eventually replied, "Well, I am Sergeant Charles Dawkins, ex- Stafford's, do I know you?"

Dennis held out his hand and said, "It's a great honour, Sergeant; unfortunately, I joined the Regiment shortly after you left and didn't have the privilege of serving under you. I just recognised you from your photograph in the Sergeants' Mess. I asked who you were, and several of the older men told me you were one of the finest soldiers to ever serve in the Regiment." Dennis noticed the look of pride on the security guard's face as he put his notebook into his pocket, came to attention and shook Dennis's hand.

Meanwhile, not far away, Stinky had spotted the cleaning lady in an adjoining room. She was wearing a long apron stained with a mixture of dirt, polish, disinfectant and tomato soup. She had a cigarette dangling from the corner of her mouth. Stinky watched her for a few minutes as she moved a pile of dust from one end of the room to the other end, using a long brush. There didn't appear to be any good reason for moving the dust. *Probably just passing the time*, he thought. Her mind seemed to be elsewhere, possibly trying to work out how she came to be doing such a fascinating job. As Stinky had suspected, she looked less like Jane Fonda and more like Henry Fonda, but still he approached, gave her his best smile and said, "I suppose you do all the work around here," and was pleasantly rewarded by the way in which her face lit up, probably just the shock of someone acknowledging her existence.

Meanwhile, Dennis and Dawkins were getting along like old mates. They had spent several moments complaining about Buckethead, whom the security guard seemed to hold personally responsible for ruining his career. He was obviously a man who held a grudge. He seemed fascinated when Dennis told him he was a Private Investigator, but as soon as Dennis asked him about the theft of the painting, he clammed up. "Sorry, Dennis," he said, "it's more than my job's worth to discuss that."

Dennis felt like he was losing him, it was time to show his renowned acting skills. He stopped in mid-sentence, glanced at his watch and shouted, "Excuse me, Charles." He pulled the cricket bat out of the sack, threw the sack to one side and to the guard's amazement, suddenly started practising his forward defensive shots. The guard was even more amazed when on the last shot, Dennis leaned too far forward and toppled over onto his face, immediately leaping up as if it were part of the procedure. Charles glanced around the room to see if anyone else had noticed, but before he could say anything, Dennis said, "Sorry about that, but my uncle told me I must practise a few forward defensive shots every hour, on the hour; evidently, that's what made him such a great player." He ignored the security guard whilst he placed the bat back into the sack, but after a few seconds, as he'd hoped, the guard asked, "Who is he then, your uncle?"

"Oh, you probably won't have heard of him," he said, and then once again removed the bat from the sack and held it up so the security guard could see the signature. Dennis watched the look of recognition appear on his face and knew he had him hooked.

He stared at the bat and muttered, "J. Smith. Is that M.J.K Smith, is he your uncle?"

"He may be M.J.K. Smith to you," Dennis said, "but to me, he will always be just Uncle Jimmy."

The security guard suddenly looked suspicious. "That's strange because his name is John, Michael John Knight Smith." He stared at Dennis, who hesitated for a moment and then said, "To the outside world perhaps, but to close friends and family, he will always be Jimmy. That's just the kind of down to earth fellow he is."

The guard slowly nodded his head and hugged the bat as if it were a religious icon. "Yes, I always knew he was a great man. Do you play, have you got the great man's genes?" he asked.

Dennis nodded.

"My forward-defensive stroke was the talk of the Dudley under twelves, it was just assumed that one day I would play for England, but then, just like your good self, I chose to serve my country in a different way."

Dawkins looked confused.

"The army," Dennis told him, "we both served in the army."

The guard nodded.

"Yes, of course, quite so, but still, he must have taught you a great deal."

"Absolutely, and not just cricket, he gave me so much advice about other things," Dennis said and then added, "He always used to say to me, 'If you can't say something nice about someone…'"

The security guard held up his hand to interrupt him.

"I know exactly what you are going to say; my late mother used to say the same thing to me, 'If you can't say something nice about someone, don't say anything at all.'"

Dennis looked surprised.

"That's strange; Uncle Jimmy used to say, 'If you can't say something nice about someone, say something nasty. Still, I suppose your mother's saying works as well."

Sometime later, Stinky stared across at his friend on the other side of the café table and said, "How did it go?"

Dennis took a sip from his cup of tea, smiled and replied, "It wasn't easy. It cost me a genuine Jemima Smith cricket bat. But, before we get to that, tell me about Jane Fonda, the cleaning lady."

Stinky smiled. "Well, she did tell me several times that she drinks in The Red Lion pub in Soho Road, Handsworth, every Friday night, just in case I ever wanted to buy her a drink."

Dennis nodded. "Good to see that even though you are now a respectable married man, you haven't lost your touch. But did she actually tell you anything useful?"

"Not really," Stinky said. "She heard a lot of shouting. Evidently, a Mrs…," Stinky studied his notebook, "A Mrs Templer discovered the theft. She's in charge of cataloguing the collections, middle-aged, wears glasses, a bit mousy, always got a mardy look on her face, according to Jane. She raised the alarm, Head of Security, Dawkins, came running and called in the police, led by DS Pratt. Evidently, Pratt is already convinced that a certain Winston Jacobs is the inside man; he worked here for a month or so as a night caretaker, but your man Dawkins sacked him when a few items went missing."

"I told you," Dennis said, "always ask the cleaning lady if you need to know something. Anything else?"

Stinky looked thoughtful. "Well, she doesn't think Winston had anything to do with it. She said he had a lovely Jamaican accent and always said good morning to her."

"Well, that's all very well," Dennis told his friend, "but I'm not sure that sort of thing would impress a judge."

Stinky started to put his notebook away into his shirt pocket but then stopped. "There was one other thing, probably just a coincidence. I asked her if she'd noticed anything unusual that morning, and she said the door to the old basement was left open. She had to draw Mr Dawkins' attention to it; he keeps the keys to all the doors in his office. I don't think there's much down there; they just use it to store cleaning products."

"And was anything missing?" Dennis asked.

Stinky shook his head. "Not as far as she could tell, not that there's anything valuable down there anyway. She did say she thought something looked different, but she couldn't tell what, and then she reminded me that she drinks in The Red Lion, just in case I need to question her further."

Dennis took a sip of tea and pulled a face. "Cold," he mumbled and then, "Don't despair, Stinky, you may get to visit The Red Lion and have that drink with Jane. Dawkins mentioned the same thing. He was checking out the basement when your Mrs Templer raised the alarm. He was surprised as he was certain he'd locked the basement door the previous day. Pratt wasn't interested as the thief appears to have smashed a window to get in and out. Strangely though, no alarm went off. Dawkins said he fired Winston Jacobs after a few items went missing on his watch, nothing much, a packet of tea, some souvenir pens, that sort of thing. He reckons he wasn't a bad lad, but evidently, Pratt got very excited about him."

"Did you get Winston's address?" Stinky asked.

"Well, I asked him about that, and he said he could tell me, but even better, he has a photo taken at the Christmas party, but it is going to cost me."

"How much?" Stinky enquired.

Dennis thought for a moment and said, "Probably another couple of bottles of brown ale. I'm pretty sure, lying next to that cricket bat. I noticed a genuine MJK Smith cricket ball. I just need to negotiate with Granddad."

Chapter 18

When Dennis got back to the office, Stinky was just putting the phone down. He looked up with a big smile on his face. "A job," he shouted, "a real, live job, a paying job. Not wasting time, looking for a stupid painting of a man with a big head, but a proper job." Then he noticed that Dennis was carrying a leather briefcase. "Wow, what's this? Very distinguished."

"I can tell when you're being sarcastic, Stinky," Dennis muttered. "It's a present from Gloria; she said it makes me look more professional." He turned around several times to model it.

"Sandwiches?" Stinky asked.

"Mainly," replied Dennis, opening the briefcase, "but today I am also carrying this," he removed a battered old cricket ball, "the actual ball that was bowled to M.J.K. Smith when he played his finest game for England."

"Is it really?" Stinky asked.

"Well, possibly," Dennis answered. "He lives in Warwickshire, the ball was found in a shed in Warwickshire, I'd say there's a very good chance. Anyway, what's this job?"

It turned out to be another couple with marriage problems, but this time, for a change, it was a Mrs Evelyn Turner who suspected her husband of seeing another woman. "Usual clues," Stinky told his friend, "claims of having to stay back after work, unexplained phone calls, recently bought himself some new underpants…"

Dennis interrupted, "New underpants, what's that got to do with it, I just bought some new y-fronts myself, and I'm not having an affair."

Stinky sighed and shook his head. "I think you will find that you need to get married first before you can have an affair and believe me, once you are married you won't be able to afford to buy frivolous things like new underpants. I'm still wearing the same pair I got issued within the army. Take it from me, if this man is off recklessly spending money on new underpants, he is up to no good."

Dennis stared at the floor for several minutes before saying, "I don't know if I'm ready for marriage, it all sounds too complicated."

"Well," Stinky said, "you may have no choice if Gloria is buying you a new briefcase. I'd say she will be expecting a proposal very soon."

Dennis looked relieved. "No, I'm okay, it's not a new briefcase. It had been lying in the lost property office at the Midland Hotel for four years. The manager said she could have it. I don't know what the rules are, but I don't think a second-hand briefcase requires a marriage proposal. Anyway, I must pop back to the Art Gallery and tempt Dawkins with this priceless cricket ball."

Stinky put his feet up on the office table and leaned back in his chair. "Well, you do that, and I better keep my eye on the telephone. Mrs Turner said she would call me back the next time her husband tells her he has to work late."

***

The Security Guard looked like he hadn't moved since Dennis had last spoken to him. He was still standing outside his office, looking like a man who'd just lost a priceless painting. Dennis walked up to him and said, "You were saying you may have something for me."

Dawkins stared back and replied, "And you were saying you may have something for me."

Dennis looked suspiciously about him, carefully opened his briefcase and removed the tattered-looking cricket ball. He held it up and said, "I was worried carrying this around in public without an armed guard. It's the ball that was bowled to him in his big game."

Dawkins gasped, "You don't mean the 121 against South Africa?"

Dennis shook his head as if in admiration, "You really are an expert on Uncle Jimmy." The Security Guard went to take the ball off Dennis, but Dennis quickly put it back into his case.

"First things first now, Sergeant Dawkins, I think you have something for me."

Dawkins opened his office door and beckoned Dennis to follow him in. He wrote '56 Patten Road, Aston' on a piece of paper and then opened a drawer in his desk, and after searching around for a few minutes pulled out a coloured photograph. "I took this at the Christmas party," he told Dennis. Dennis studied the photo. There was a large table with several bottles of drinks on top and some plates of sandwiches scattered around. A woman and three men stared back at Dawkins, who no doubt had just announced 'Say cheese'. The woman and two of the men looked so bored that they seemed to be struggling with the entire cheese saying concept, but the young man nearest the camera, obviously Winston, seemed to be having the time of his life. He appeared to be screaming 'Cheese' back at the camera. "What is he like?" Dennis asked.

Dawkins thought for a moment. "Six-foot tall, about twenty-one years old, Jamaican, with a smile like a watermelon."

Dennis shook his head and said, "No, I mean what sort of a person is he?"

Dawkins sighed. "Oh, he's not a bad lad. A couple of items went missing; I had no choice but to sack him. I'd be amazed if he had anything to do with this though, even though DS Pratt seems to think he's involved."

Dennis put the photo into his briefcase and watched as Dawkins held his hand out. "Well, that's all very interesting," he told the guard, "but as you yourself say, this cricket ball is the very one used in Uncle Jimmy's most famous innings. I really think I deserve one more favour."

***

Stinky picked the phone up on its second ring. "Hello, Blackshaw and Bisskit, Private Investigators."

There were some moments' pause and then he heard Dennis say, "I think you will find that it's actually 'Bisskit and Blackshaw Private Investigators'."

Stinky laughed. "How did it go with grumpy Dawkins?"

"Not bad," Dennis told him, "he's going to let me have a look around the old basement in a minute. He says nothing's missing, but I'd still like to check it out myself. Anyway, don't worry about that. I was thinking; you really should take Brenda out for the afternoon; she's always stuck inside the house. Why don't you take a bit of money out of petty cash and get the bus out to Aston, take her to Aston Hall, it's a lovely old building. Do you know there is still a hole in the big staircase made by a cannonball, hundreds of years ago?"

It was the "take some money out of petty cash" that immediately alerted Stinky. "What's the catch?" he asked.

"Catch! No catch," Dennis told him, "but I was thinking, whilst Brenda is checking out the cannonball damage, you could pop around the corner to 56, Patten Road and see if there's any sign of young Winston Jacobs. Evidently, he's six feet tall, about twenty-one years old and Jamaican, with a smile like a watermelon. I've got a photo of him at a Christmas party."

"That's not much use to me," Stinky complained, "Unless you can somehow shove the photograph down the telephone line. How am I supposed to recognise him?"

"Well, I'm no expert," Dennis said, "But I should imagine he is the only six feet, twenty-one-year-old Jamaican with a smile like a watermelon, living at 56 Patten Road Aston." The phone suddenly went dead, and Stinky reached for the petty cash box.

***

Dennis followed Dawkins down steps and several corridors, past displays and exhibitions, then down another set of concrete steps and past a large room. He noticed a big solid door with a heavy padlock on it. "That's the basement," the Security Guard told him. "We store a lot of stuff in there, paintings, antiques, that sort of thing, that's why it's locked up, the keys kept in my office."

Dennis looked surprised. "I thought you said there was nothing valuable kept in the basement."

Dawkins continued walking down to the far end of the corridor. "That's the new basement there; I was referring to the old basement." At the end of the corridor, he turned left, and they walked down another set of steep steps that had worn down over the years. At the bottom was an old door. Dawkins put a key in the lock and opened it. "This is the original basement, on the old foundations." He pulled a cord just inside the door, and a dull light came on. "It's too damp down here to keep anything valuable, so we use it to store cleaning materials, maintenance stuff, that sort of thing." Dennis walked down yet more steps and looked out into a surprisingly large room. He could hardly make out the far walls in the gloom. He could feel the damp in the air. Looking around he saw several drums stacked on the floor. He could make out 'polish' labels on some and 'disinfectant' on others. There were also shelves with tools stacked on them, saws, hammers, boxes of nails. There were planks of wood and display cabinets stacked against one of the walls. On the other side, some old rolls of carpet. "As I said," Dawkins muttered, "there's nothing worth pinching down here. The door just got accidentally left open, that's all."

Dennis gave the room one last look and nodded, maybe the guard was right. Dawkins locked up and held out his hand, "Now," he said, "I believe you have something for me."

Chapter 19

"It's nice to get out of the house," Brenda said. "Not sure why we had to come to Aston Hall though, I have been here twice before."

Stinky held her hand. "Well, so have I, my dear, but I was just sitting in the office and thought we hadn't seen it together, and I know how you like looking at old furniture."

Brenda looked baffled. "Not sure where you got that idea from, we have a house full of old furniture, some of it older than they have here."

But Stinky seemed distracted and kept glancing at his watch. Eventually, he said, "Oh look, there's a café over there, why don't you order us a cuppa. I've just got to pop and see someone. I'll be back in a minute." Brenda turned to ask him where he was going, but he was already disappearing out of the door.

Patten Road proved to be further away than Dennis had indicated. Stinky ran most of the way and was panting as he counted the numbers towards 56. The houses seemed fairly run-down in this part of Aston. He passed number 40, looked up the road and immediately leapt behind a tree. A police car was parked outside a house. Another car pulled in next to it, and DS Pratt climbed out and adjusted his jacket. Stinky couldn't walk up and see what was going on because he knew Pratt was bound to recognise him and want to know what he was doing there. So instead, he walked down a side street to his left. A short distance up the street there was a narrow lane to his right; it ran behind the houses, so he turned and walked down it. Seconds later, he heard a scraping noise ahead of him, a creaky old gate suddenly opened, and a six foot, twenty-one-year-old Jamaican, with a smile like a watermelon, stepped furtively out into the lane. He was wearing an Aston Villa top and carrying a rucksack over his shoulder. He looked down the lane and seemed to relax, then he turned and saw Stinky striding towards him and nearly fell over. Quickly regaining his composure, he took off down the lane at great speed. Stinky raced after him, feeling confident that he would soon catch up. As long as he could remember, he'd had been a good runner. When he was young, it had been a necessity because grown-ups were always chasing him, following some act of naughtiness, and then, once he joined the army, he had realised just how good a runner he was. Whilst others, especially Dennis, were complaining about every run and march, Stinky loved it, the further, the better.

Winston ran down the lane and eventually across a road and into a park, he kept looking back and could see the man getting closer.

Stinky was only a few feet behind when it suddenly occurred to him that Winston may turn violent. Stinky could handle himself in a fight, but Winston was quite a big lad. Suddenly, as he passed a park bench, Winston stopped, dropped his rucksack to the ground and sat down.

"I'm a lover, not a fighter," he gasped and smiled a smile as big as a watermelon.

"Me too," Stinky told him, and held out his hand, "My name's Stinky, and yours is Winston."

"Stinky?" he enquired as he shook his hand.

Stinky smiled. "I hated washing when I was younger."

Winston nodded. "Me too, the only time I washed was when I went swimming in the river." Then he looked serious and said, "Look, you seem a nice man, Stinky, can you tell the landlord that I wasn't at home. I'll pay next week, definitely."

Now, it was Stinky's turn to look serious. "Landlord? I'm nothing to do with your landlord."

Winston looked relieved. "Oh, when I heard the loud banging I thought it was Dempster, my landlord, he's a bit upset 'cause I'm a week behind on my rent."

Stinky shook his head. "No, that loud banging you heard was the police, they are probably searching the house now."

The watermelon smile had completely disappeared. "Police? What do they want? I haven't done anything."

"Well, I'm guessing that they want to ask you what you know about The Man from Paris with the Very Large Head," Stinky told him.

Winston looked totally confused. "What man from Paris?" he asked, "I don't know anyone with a big head. My friend Leroy has got big ears, but his head's okay."

Stinky prided himself on being able to read people, and he knew that Winston wasn't bluffing. He genuinely didn't have a clue what Stinky was talking about. Stinky told him all about the theft of the painting and how he and his partner were investigating it. "Wow, it just shows I should read the papers now and again," he said. The watermelon smile was back. "I only worked there for a while, then Dawkins sacked me. He said I'd pinched stuff, but I swear I hadn't. It was a rubbish job anyway; I hated working there at night, it was spooky; sometimes I would hear strange noises."

They sat enjoying the sunshine for a minute, and then Stinky sighed and said, "Well, I better get back to Aston Hall, I left my wife queuing up for a cuppa about an hour ago, I'm in big trouble,"

Winston laughed. "So, you're a Private Investigator, is it just like the movies?"

Now, Stinky laughed. "Yes, exactly the same, except we don't appear to earn any money."

Winston looked disappointed. "But do you get beautiful women walk into your office begging you for help?"

Stinky shook his head. "Hasn't happened yet, but as my friend often says to me, 'Its early days yet, Stinky.'"

They both stood at the same time and shook hands. "I'd keep out of the way for a few days until this painting business is cleared up," Winston told him that he'd been on his way to stay with a friend down south when he'd left the house. He walked off in one direction and Stinky went in the opposite direction, running towards Aston Hall as quickly as he could and trying to work out how to explain his absence for the last hour to Brenda.

Chapter 20

"So, we can forget all about Winston then," Dennis said.

"Yes, he didn't have a clue what I was talking about," Stinky told him.

Dennis had known Stinky for a long time, and if he said Winston wasn't involved in the theft, that was good enough for him.

"Still, at least the day wasn't wasted, you will be in the good books with Brenda after taking her out."

"Well, that's where you are wrong," Stinky replied. "In fact, far from being in the good books, I am in the very bad books, mainly for leaving her sitting with a pot of tea whilst I disappeared for an hour. Not only that, but I've just had to tell her that I'm going to be out this evening. Mrs Turner rang up to tell me that her husband has just been in touch. Evidently, he has to work late tonight."

Dennis looked surprised. "See, that's what I don't understand about women. You do your best, and you still get into trouble. Anyway, the problem we have now is that with Winston in the clear, we are right back where we started from. I suppose I could go and have another word with Dawkins; the trouble is, I am completely out of M.J.K. Smith memorabilia."

"I may be able to help you there," Stinky told him, "I was clearing out some old junk the other day, and I found my old cricket stumps."

Dennis looked up, "Could they possibly be M.J.K. Smith's old cricket stumps? The stumps he batted in front of as a youth. The very stumps that made him the player he is today?"

"Well, I found them at the rubbish tip, so it's not beyond the bounds of possibility," Stinky replied.

"That's good enough for me, bring them in tomorrow," Dennis said and then suddenly groaned. "Oh no, I've just remembered, I won't be in until late afternoon; I've promised to help Dad with Miss Plunge's funeral."

Stinky looked concerned. "Are you sure that's a good idea, Ginge. You know you are a bit accident-prone. The way I see it, funerals are very similar to weddings, and you know what happened when you were Best Man at my wedding." Just in case Dennis had forgotten, Stinky reminded him. "You accidentally locked yourself in the freezer and not only missed the reception, but almost froze to death."

Dennis looked thoughtful for a moment and then muttered, "I'll be fine," and then more forcefully, "I'll be fine. I know I had the odd disaster in the past, but that is all behind me now, Stinky. No, I feel very confident that it will go fine, everyone will have a good time. Well, apart from Miss Plunge, I don't suppose she will enjoy it much."

Chapter 21

24 Hours Later

Stinky shook his head. "You must be exaggerating; surely it can't have been all that bad."

Dennis held his head in his hands. "I only wish I was, Stinky, I only wish I was exaggerating."

***

It had been announced that Miss Petunia Plunge, former Haberdasher and Akela to The Dudley Wolf Cubs, had sadly passed away. It had brought back many memories for Dennis. He had never been one of her favourite cubs, but he felt that she had helped to prepare him for his later military career. In fact, now that he thought about it, she had run the Wolf Pack in a very similar manner to the way in which Buckethead had run the Regiment. Still, he held no hard feelings and was sad to hear the news from his father, which explained why he had felt unable to refuse his father's request for assistance at the funeral. It turned out that there were two funerals that day. Unfortunately, a couple of workers were off sick, leaving Mr Bisskit in a bit of a mess. Dennis had eventually agreed to take the morning off work and help out. "Nothing technical," his dad had assured him, "just follow my lead and you can't go wrong."

His father looked him up and down. Dennis was wearing his blue suit and a black tie. Mr Bisskit shook his head sadly. "A blue suit, it's not really appropriate, could we paint it black?"

"No, we could not paint it black," Dennis told him, "it's my only suit. Anyway, the paint would just peel off when it dried."

"What about that ginger hair, could you dye that black?" Dennis sighed and shook his head, so his dad left the room and seconds later returned with his old, black trilby. "Here, you can wear this. I suppose that will have to do."

They drove slowly to Nutter's Funeral Home. Dennis kept tutting and glancing at his watch because his father had taken to driving his car at ten miles an hour as if he were heading a funeral procession. "More haste, less speed," he said eventually, responding to his son's mutterings.

"I've never understood that," Dennis said, "it makes no sense; if there is more haste, surely there will be more speed, not less." He stared at his father, but Mr Bisskit didn't seem to want to discuss it further.

They finally arrived at the back entrance of Nutters and entered the building. It was unnaturally quiet. "Looks like we have the place to ourselves." Mr Bisskit said, glancing at his pocket watch. "The other funeral should be starting about now. We better get busy, people will start arriving in half an hour or so to follow Miss Plunge to her resting place." Dennis had visions of people following all the way to the grave and leaping in like lemmings, but he assumed they didn't follow her quite that far.

His father turned on some lights and then solemnly opened the door to the viewing room. Dennis followed him in, and then suddenly stopped, realising there was an open coffin on a table in the centre of the room. "Is that Miss Plunge?" he gasped.

"I certainly hope so," his father stated. "If it isn't, we are in big trouble." It smelt a bit musty in the room, so Mr Bisskit grabbed a long wooden pole with a hook on the end of it and opened a couple of the high windows to let some air in. He turned and looked at his son. "Okay, Dennis, you do what you have to do, I will be preparing the hearse." Earlier that day, he had been telling Dennis how some people left little mementoes in the coffins: poems, photos of loved ones, etc. Dennis had asked if it would be okay for him to place his Wolf Cubs Basic Knot Tying Badge alongside her body, as a tribute. Now he was alone in the room. He hesitatingly approached the coffin, and there she lay. Someone had dressed her up smartly and applied more make-up than he had ever seen her wearing before. She was wearing a long, black skirt and blue, frilly blouse; on her head was her best Sunday hat. She looked in a lot better mood in death than she ever had in life. Dennis had always wondered why Miss Plunge had become Akela in the Dudley Cubs; she had never married and certainly didn't like children, especially Dennis. But his mother had kindly pointed out to him, "Don't take it badly, Son, it's nothing personal, she dislikes men, women, and children equally."

He pulled his wallet out of his suit pocket. He'd put the badge in there for safe keeping, but as he leaned towards the coffin, a two-shilling coin fell out of the wallet, bounced off Miss Plunge's chin and rolled down the front of her blouse. Dennis just stood there; he couldn't believe it. He leaned closer and went to lift her blouse slightly, but he just couldn't bring himself to do it. As he turned, he let out a cry and leapt back. Miss Plunge's right eye had suddenly opened and was staring at him. He looked around and saw a pair of black gloves lying nearby, so he put them on and closed the offending eyelid. "Sorry about this, Miss Plunge," he whispered, but as soon as he moved away the eyelid opened again. After several attempts, he gave up and pulled her hat down over her face. He undid the top button of her blouse, but couldn't bring himself to go any further. Looking around the room, he suddenly had an idea. He grabbed the long, wooden pole with the hook on the end that his dad had used to open the windows; the pole was about eight feet long. He stood back behind Miss Plunge's head and reached forward with the pole, slowly sliding it down the front of her blouse. Then he quickly pulled it back, hoping to flick the coin out, but there was no sign of his two shillings. He tried again, but when he pulled it back, he was horrified to find that the hook had caught on something. He gently tugged it a couple of times to no avail, but then, worrying in case his father returned, he got a good grip on the end of the pole with both hands and pulled with all his might. Suddenly, there was a loud twanging noise, like the sound his old catapult used to make when he fired it. Next thing, Dennis flew backwards and ended up lying on the floor, when he looked up, Miss Plunge's hefty white brassiere was hanging from the hook. Just at that moment, Mr Bisskit entered the room and nearly fainted. "Oh, my god, Dennis, what have you done?" he cried.

Dennis cast the pole and underwear to one side scrambling to his feet, "It's not what it looks like, Dad. I dropped two shillings down Miss Plunge's blouse; the pole got stuck."

Mr Bisskit looked aghast. "It's number two in the Rule Book, do not interfere with the corpse. It's one of the important ones." He unhooked the bra from the end of the pole and stood looking at Miss Plunge for a while. "Well, obviously, I can't put it back on, it's more than my job's worth." Then he had an idea. "How much money have you got on you?"

Dennis checked his wallet; he found another three shillings. "I have five shillings, counting the other two," he pointed down Akela's blouse.

Mr Bisskit nodded. "Wait here, Mrs Ramsbottom has just come in, she's our cleaner, I will offer her five shillings to sort it out."

Mrs Ramsbottom stared at the bra, and then stared at Dennis and made the sign of the cross. He handed her the coins and said, "The other two shillings are down there somewhere; I dropped them down Miss Plunge." She shook her head and looked disgusted. Mrs Ramsbottom played Bingo alongside Dennis's mother every Friday night, and he was pretty sure what the topic of conversation would be this coming Friday. She moved towards the body, then stopped and shouted, "Get out," at Dennis and his father.

***

Stinky stared back open-mouthed. "Wow, I genuinely thought that you could never surprise me, Ginge," he said, "but this time you have surpassed yourself. Even by your own high standards that is a disaster. I presume that was the end of your undertaking career?"

Dennis had been holding his head in his hands, but he looked up and said, "Well, no, he needed my assistance. Anyway, that was only the start; things went downhill after that."

***

The door flew open, and Mrs Ramsbottom exited, slamming it behind her. "She looks as good as she's going to look, except her one eye won't shut," she said. She gave Dennis one last glance, muttered something in Latin and strode quickly away.

Dennis and his father entered the room. "There's no one wants to view the coffin so we can put the lid on."

They stared down at the body, and the open eye stared back. "I've never seen that sort of thing before, Son, it's not normal." Mr Bisskit mumbled.

Dennis suddenly had an idea. He took the bubble-gum he was chewing out of his mouth, placed it on Miss Plunge's lower eyelid and stuck the top eyelid down on to it. Mr Bisskit nodded and quickly dropped the lid on top of the coffin and commenced screwing it down. He then brushed down his suit and put on his black Top Hat. After that, they went and checked out the front of the funeral home. Miss Plunge had been a spinster all her life and had no family that anyone knew about. Dennis hadn't really met anyone who had a good word for her, and yet there were still about twenty people waiting beside their cars, ready to follow the hearse to Dudley Cemetery. Mr Bisskit recognised some regulars who came to all the funerals, even if they didn't know the deceased, it was just a day out. "We are just going to put Miss Plunge into the hearse; we will be here in about five minutes if you would all like to be ready in your vehicles. Let me remind you; we travel at ten miles an hour, it's not a race to see who can reach the cemetery first."

Mr Bisskit suddenly realised there was a problem. The door leading from the viewing room to the backyard where the hearse was parked had been locked, and he couldn't find the key anywhere. He walked off and came back wheeling a large coffin carrier, as he called it. It was basically a wooden base on top of four large wheels, on the side of which was a long handle which operated the brake. He grabbed hold of one end of the coffin containing Miss Plunge and instructed Dennis to lift the other end. They positioned the coffin in the centre of the carrier and pushed it through a door onto an alleyway which ran down the side of the funeral home and out onto a side road. "You wait here and guard the coffin, Son; I'm leaving you in charge. I'll nip around and get the hearse. We can load it on here and then drive around to the front to meet the mourners."

Dennis used his hand to flatten his thinning hair down and then quickly placed the trilby on his head before the wind could destroy his good work. He thought he would line the carrier up more closely to the kerb, so he pulled the handle up and pushed against it; he was surprised by just how easily it shot forward. He suddenly realised it had been parked on a bit of a slope, so he tugged the brake handle back down. There was a whining sound and a crash as something metallic fell on to the road, then the handle came away in his hand. Dennis just stared at it for a moment; then when he glanced up, he was horrified to see the coffin carrier slowly rolling downhill. He raced after it and grabbed hold of the back of the carrier, but it was too heavy and just dragged him along. It started to pick up speed. Dennis remembered his father's words, "I'm leaving you in charge". He had to stay with Miss Plunge, so he raced after it as quickly as he could, and when he caught up, he jumped onto the back and climbed on to the coffin.

Mr Bisskit drove the hearse slowly around the corner, whistling a Frank Sinatra song he was fond of. He was just thinking how nice it was to have father and son working together when he saw a strange sight. Miss Plunge was hurtling down the hill on the back of the coffin carrier, with Dennis sitting astride the coffin as if he were riding in the Grand National.

The black trilby blew away in the wind, and Dennis struggled to hold on to the coffin with one hand whilst holding his hair flat with the other. It crossed his mind that it would be just his luck to pass Gloria whilst his hair was doing its own thing.

Having time on his hands, he decided to review his situation. He was riding a coffin down a steep hill, with no way of stopping. If the carrier maintained its present course, he would reach the bottom of the hill and cross a busy road within a couple of minutes. Fortunately, at that moment, Fate lent a hand. Mr Todger, his old maths teacher, stepped out of his car, spotted his old pupil, waved and shouted, "Good morning, Dennis, lovely day."

Even though Dennis was, at the time, riding a coffin down a steep hill whilst hanging on with one hand and trying to keep some sense of decorum to his hairstyle with the other, he felt obligated to wave back. It required a rapid decision on which hand to use. He chose to maintain his dignity and use the hand he was gripping the coffin with. The carrier seemed to sense this slight movement and veered violently to the right, heading in the general direction of number 46 Arcadia Avenue, home of a Mrs,

Gladys Bouvier. There was a low wall in front of the garden of number 46, and, on striking it, the coffin carrier came to a sudden halt. Unfortunately, Dennis, the coffin and Miss Plunge did not. The coffin flew through the air with Dennis sitting astride it, looking from a distance like The Lone Ranger riding his trusty horse, Silver. At that moment, Mrs Bouvier, whom it turned out was partially deaf, was busy hanging out the washing and failed to hear Dennis's cries for help. In fact, the first she saw of him was when he parted company with the flying coffin halfway across the front garden, bounced, rolled over several times and came to rest at her feet. Meanwhile, the coffin did a couple of spectacular somersaults, the lid flew off, and Miss Plunge was catapulted through the air, landing next to Mrs Bouvier. Remarkably, she landed on her feet, and just stood there for a second or two, just long enough for Mrs Bouvier to glance over and say, "Is that you, Miss Plunge, I didn't hear you come in. Someone told me you were not well." Then the dearly departed former leader of the Dudley Wolf Pack slowly toppled over, like a tree being uprooted in a storm, and landed directly on top of Dennis. Their noses touched. He watched as the top eyelid of her right eye slowly unglued itself from the bubble-gum on her lower lid and sprang open, staring disapprovingly at her tormentor.

On the front-page editorial of the following week's Dudley Times, it was reported that Dennis and Mrs Bouvier's screams could be heard across most of Dudley.

***

Stinky stared at his friend. Nothing would ever surprise him again. "I'll tell you one thing, Ginge," he said, smiling, "Miss Plunge has had more excitement since she died than she ever had whilst alive."

But Dennis was not in the mood. "It's not funny, Stinky, I saw things yesterday that no man should ever see; I had nightmares last night. There are some things once seen, cannot be unseen." Stinky asked what happened next, so Dennis explained to him how his father had driven after him, closely followed by the convoy of cars containing the mourners who had driven around the block to see what was going on. The entire convoy had to stop halfway down the hill, whilst Mr Bisskit leapt out of the hearse to retrieve his black trilby which had blown off Dennis's head. Once they all arrived at number 46, they shoved Miss Plunge back into the coffin and carried it to the hearse. Of course, the Coffin Carrier was ruined; one of the wheels had fallen off. A neighbour said she would stay with Mrs Bouvier, who was in shock until the doctor arrived.

Stinky started to get up from the table, so Dennis asked him where he was going, "Well, I presume that was it, that was the end of your career as an undertaker."

"I wish," Dennis told him. "No such luck. Things got worse after that."

"We reached the cemetery, and the rain started, it absolutely poured down," Dennis continued. "My suit got drenched, the trilby didn't help much. Everyone kept staring at me, even the vicar as if the word had got around that I'd had a couple of unfortunate incidents. Anyway, we lowered Miss Plunge into the grave, and we all walked away, but I felt that I had to go back and apologise to her. I know it sounds silly, Stinky, but I just felt that I'd let her down somehow. Anyway, I leaned over the grave to speak, and next thing, I'm sliding in the mud and dropping down there."

Stinky was shaking, trying not to laugh.

"I landed on the edge of the coffin; the lid flew open, I had to have a quick look."

Dennis hesitated, so Stinky asked, "What, Dennis, what did you see?"

Eventually, his friend explained, "Her eye had come open again, the bubble-gum was stuck on the end of her nose, and she was staring at me. It was evil, Stinky as if she were taunting me as if she were saying 'you never deserved that Basic Knot Tying Badge'. I pushed the lid back down and sat on the coffin. Eventually, the gravediggers came along to fill the grave in. They nearly had a heart attack when I shouted; they thought it was Miss Plunge wanting a second opinion. One of them tried to pull me out, but then he fell in. The other went for help and eventually we were both pulled out."

Stinky shook his head in disbelief.

"My suit was completely ruined," Dennis added, "I never noticed until later that one of my trouser legs had fallen off. When I ran back to the grave to retrieve it, it was too late; they had already filled it in." Dennis seemed surprised when Stinky asked why no one had mentioned to him earlier that he had a complete trouser leg missing. "Maybe they just thought it was some sort of fashion statement," he said.

Stinky was reluctant even to bother asking, but eventually, he did, "Surely that is it, surely that's the end of your undertaking career?"

"Oh, absolutely," Dennis replied. "The thing was, I also left Dad's black trilby in the grave. He said it was just too stressful working with me; I can never work with him again. Now, I must buy a new suit, and I owe Dad for a new trilby, not to mention the fact that I had to pay Mrs Ramsbottom five shillings to put Miss Plunge back together again."

Stinky tried to cheer him up. "You know, my friend, it strikes me that being a Private Investigator is a lot safer than being an undertaker."

Dennis nodded in agreement and said, "I'd go even further, Stinky. I would say that even when we were in the Regiment, getting shot at in Uganda, it was still a lot safer than being an undertaker."

"Well, here's something to cheer you up," Stinky said, and handed his friend a battered looking set of cricket stumps.

"Oh, good," Dennis said, "are those M.J.K. Smith's originals?"

"More than likely," Stinky replied. "Almost definitely, very possibly, there's a remote chance anyway. Now, the other big news is that it's not looking good for Mr Turner." He removed his notebook from his jacket pocket and proceeded to tell his friend what had happened the previous evening.

"I waited outside his office. At precisely six-thirty, he left the office with a Miss Watkins, aged twenty-one, she has been his secretary for the last three months. I watched as they walked down the alleyway at the side of the building, and, before they got into the same car, they kissed passionately."

Dennis interrupted, "Passionately, you say?"

Stinky checked his notes. "Yes, I would definitely describe it as passionately."

Dennis nodded thoughtfully. "Carry on."

"I followed them to The Britannia Hotel in Wolverhampton, they kissed passionately again, before entering the hotel, and booked in under the name Smith," Stinky explained that he knew the bellboy there, as he'd paid him for information before.

"Nice work, Stinky," Dennis said.

Stinky continued, "I waited in the car, and at approximately 9 pm, they left the hotel, kissing passionately again before getting into Mr Turner's car. The traffic was so bad that I couldn't follow them, so I went back to the hotel and checked with my bellboy. He said that Mr Turner had paid for the night, but after a few hours, had then said something had come up, and they would have to leave. On my way home, I drove past the Turners' house and noticed that Mr Turner's car was now parked out the front, so I went home."

Dennis considered all this information for a moment and then said, "Well, you may call me overly suspicious here, my friend but, and as you know, I hate to think badly of anyone, but, I do believe Mrs Turner may have some reason to be concerned. I think you may have to tell her the unfortunate news."

Stinky nodded, but Dennis noticed that he seemed hesitant, so asked him what was wrong.

"Oh, nothing, it's just that Mrs Turner did say that money was no object, it didn't matter how long it took, she just wanted to know the truth."

Dennis suddenly understood what his friend was getting at. "Money's no object, you say. It doesn't matter how long it takes."

Stinky nodded. "Well, I suppose we shouldn't rush into things."

Dennis told him, "Let's face it, there could be a perfectly innocent explanation for Mr Turner kissing his secretary passionately, and then booking into a hotel under a false name with her."

"Absolutely," Stinky agreed, "I can't actually think of anything offhand, but who are we to cast aspersions on what, as you say, could be a perfectly innocent evening."

"Very true," Dennis said. "I think, just to be on the safe side, we should keep our eyes on Mr Turner for another day or so." Then he picked up M.J.K. Smith's possible cricket stumps and added, "I better pop back to the Art Gallery and see what information I can get for these."

Stinky nodded. "Well, I'll see you in the morning, Ginge. Meanwhile, I better let Mrs Turner know that our enquiries are continuing and it could take a while." Then, as Dennis started to leave, Stinky shouted, "You'll be needing these," and handed his friend a couple of cricket bails.

"M.J.K. Smith's personal bails?" Dennis asked.

"Absolutely, almost definitely, possibly," Stinky replied.

Chapter 22

At 5pm, just as Stinky was about to leave the office, the phone rang, it was Dennis. "Old Dawkins was very excited about M.J.K. Smith's stumps he kept caressing them; it was almost creepy."

Stinky laughed. "I presume you drove a hard bargain."

"I didn't need to, he already had a list of four people who have suddenly left the employment of the Art Gallery and Museum over the last year, and their addresses for us to check."

Stinky was quiet for so long that eventually, Dennis asked if he was still there.

"Just thinking," he mumbled.

"It's just a thought, but what if Dawkins is the inside man, or even did the theft on his own. It's funny that he has four names already for you. He would know that would keep you busy and out of his way for a while."

Now it was Dennis's turn to be quiet for a while before saying, "No, I can't see it. After all, he's ex Staffordshire Regiment."

"Well, just because we are a credit to the Regiment, it doesn't mean everyone is," Stinky told his friend. "He may have started off okay, and just gone a bit strange over the years."

"What, do you mean, like Buckethead?" Dennis asked.

"No, that's completely different," Stinky explained. "He was born strange and then got even stranger over the years. Look at it this way. Dawkins is in a perfect position. He comes and goes as he wants; he holds all the keys. He could easily have gone to work early and smuggled the painting out."

Dennis thought about this. Stinky was right, Dawkins had already sent them after Winston, and now four other ex-employees. He knew who Dennis and Stinky were investigating, and he also knew what the police were up to. He could just carry on until the case went cold and then sell the painting, or he may already have a buyer.

"You're right, my friend, I think we better start checking out his movements, starting tonight."

"I'm afraid you're on your own," Stinky told him, "I'm busy watching Mr Turner, it turns out he's got to work late again."

Dennis groaned down the phone. "You know I'm no good on my own; I'll fall asleep."

Stinky had an idea, "Ask Gloria; she might want to accompany you. Take a flask and some sandwiches; you can make a date of it."

Dennis wasn't sure. "I suppose I could ask. You and I are highly trained professionals, but as long as she just sat there and did exactly as I say, I don't suppose anything could go wrong."

Stinky smiled to himself. It had all the makings of a Dennis disaster.

Chapter 23

Surprisingly, Gloria had not only welcomed his offer to accompany him for the evening, but as they sat in his car, watching the house where ex-Sergeant Dawkins lived, he realised she actually found it exciting. Normally, when they had to do this job, Dennis had trouble keeping his eyes open, but Gloria could hardly keep still, she kept looking up and down the street, until eventually, she asked, "What exactly are we looking for?"

Dennis shook his head. "I'm not sure, to be honest. Maybe Dawkins is completely innocent, but we may be lucky, someone suspicious looking visits him, or he visits someone else. Obviously, what would be best is if he walks out of his house carrying The Man from Paris with The Very Large Head, but I don't suppose that will happen." Secretly, Dennis suspected they were wasting their time, but still, Gloria seemed impressed.

She suddenly smiled and said, "You know what this reminds me of, a James Bond film."

Dennis sat up straight in his seat, breathed in until his chest had expanded as far as it could, and then said, "Funny you should say that. I am often referred to as the James Bond of Dudley, in fact, I was considering dying my hair black, like Sean Connery."

She looked shocked and shouted, "No, don't do that, I love your ginger hair," then she leaned over to run her fingers through it, but Dennis was having none of that, he had spent 30 minutes that evening carefully combing it. So, he leapt backwards shouting, "I think I saw something." Amazingly, at that moment, the front door of Dawkins' house opened, and he stepped out, glancing suspiciously up and down the street. They both shrank down in their seats, even though Dennis had parked well away from the street lamp. The security guard commenced walking down the road. Dennis waited until he was some distance off but still in sight, started the car engine and slowly followed. When he walked past the bus shelter and carried on, Dennis said, "Wherever he is heading, it looks like he's going to walk there, we better park up and follow on foot." He pulled over to the kerb, and they quickly got out as the security guard disappeared around a bend. They ran to the corner and spotted him about thirty yards in front of them. Hearing their footsteps, he turned. Gloria immediately pushed Dennis against a wall, threw her arms around his shoulders and kissed him. Dawkins spotted the courting couple, shrugged and walked on. Gloria eventually released Dennis. "He nearly spotted us, I had to improvise," she whispered.

"Ver, ver, very good, excellent ther, thinking," Dennis gasped. They continued down the street and then watched Dawkins suddenly disappear to the right. When they reached the spot, they noticed a narrow lane. At the end of the lane was a row of four small lock-up sheds with big wooden doors, the door to the lockup on the far right, was just closing. They slowly crept along, keeping to the shadows. There was a street lamp where they had entered the lane but has they got further on, Dennis was pleased to see it was quite dark. Dark enough that they could now see the light escaping from underneath the door of the lock-up Dawkins had entered.

There was an area of waste ground next to the lock-ups. An old car with a broken windscreen was parked on it. It was the perfect spot to observe from. After a few minutes, Dennis whispered, "I wish I had bought the flask and sandwiches, we could have had a picnic." He could see her smile even in the dim light; then she suddenly jumped as an owl hooted in the distance.

Dennis chuckled and said.

"No need to be afraid, my granddad always says that wild animals are more scared of you than you are of them."

Gloria was quiet for a moment before she said.

"Well, that's not true. What about a lion? I'm pretty sure that I'm more scared of a lion than it is of me. Or a snake, or a large spider, or a leopard, or a wild dog, or a hippopotamus, or a vulture, that could peck you very badly, or a bee, that could sting you."

Dennis turned. He was going to tell her not to be silly, but as he thought more about it, he changed his mind and instead said,

"You're quite right; Granddad's an idiot."

Suddenly, she said, "We need to get closer, we may be able to hear something; I'll go and have a listen."

Dennis was horrified. "No way, you wait here, I'll go." But she quickly pointed out that Dawkins knew him, whereas he had never met her. She could walk past, and if he came out, she could just pretend she lived nearby. He knew it made sense, so reluctantly told her, "Okay, just a quick listen, but be careful." Before he had finished speaking, she was already on her way. Dennis peeped over the top of the car bonnet. Gloria was creeping closer and closer to the lockup. When she was in front of the doors, she stopped and leaned closer. Dennis could tell she was listening. After a while, he started to get concerned and spent some time trying in vain to make a sound like an owl, to attract her attention. He was just thinking it sounded less like an owl and more like an old man drowning in the canal, when suddenly, Gloria leapt back and ran around the side of the building. A second later, the large wooden door was pushed open. A man stepped out and looked around. There was no way of knowing if it was Dawkins or not as the man was wearing a balaclava which covered his face, and on top of that, a motorcycle helmet. He also wore a long heavy coat. He disappeared back into the lockup and shortly after, re-emerged, pushing a large motorbike. After locking the door, he sat astride the bike and the peace and quiet of the night was suddenly shattered as he started the engine. He sat there for a moment and then slowly moved off down the lane, before accelerating away, until he was out of sight and only the noise from the loud engine remained and then after a few moments, even that had gone, and the peace and quiet resumed.

Dennis ran from behind the wrecked car and immediately spotted Gloria emerging from the shadows. She put a finger up to her lips and shushed him before he could shout. "I'm not sure if there is someone else in there," she whispered. "I could hear voices, but I'm not sure if it's a radio. Then I heard someone walking towards the door, so I ran. Could you see if it was Dawkins?"

Dennis shook his head. "There's was no way to tell, but it was about his height." He crept to the door and leaned forward just as Gloria had done. A moment later, he stood up and said, "I think it is the radio, but can't be sure." Gloria had a better idea,

105

she walked up to the door and banged on it as loudly as possible. When no one answered, Dennis, asked what she would have done if someone had come out.

"I would just have said I was lost and looking for my dad who has a lock up around here," she calmly answered. Dennis nodded, she was good at this.

Dennis took the small torch out of his jacket pocket and examined the padlock on the door. Gloria leaned towards him. "Are you going to pick the lock, like James Bond does?"

Dennis had no idea how you would even go about picking a lock; he had just checked to see that it was definitely locked. "Obviously, normally I would," he said, "but I must have left my lock picking kit in my other jacket." He stepped back and looked around him; he noticed that the lock-ups had a flat roof, he checked around the corner and spotted a dustbin standing against the wall. "Let's check out the roof," he told Gloria, "there may be a way in."

Dennis stood on top of the dustbin and stretched up with his arms but could barely reach the roof. Gloria told him to get down. "I'm taller than you; I'll go first." Dennis was dismayed to realise that she seemed to be taking control and felt even worse when she managed to pull herself up onto the roof with seemingly little effort. "I'll pull you up," she shouted. Dennis stood on top of the dustbin with his hands raised, she reached down grabbed his wrists, and before he knew it, he was sitting on the tin roof.

"Wow, you're stronger than you look," he told her admiringly.

Gloria smiled, "I should be, Dad's had me doing push-ups since I was two years old."

Dennis stepped out to the centre of the roof and shone his torch around, he was hoping there would be some sort of skylight, but unfortunately, all he saw was a flat tin roof. "Oh well, it was worth a try," he muttered. He turned back, and at that instant, there was a loud crash, and he found himself falling. He landed heavily on top of a pile of cardboard boxes, and a split second later, Gloria landed on top of him. Amazingly, apart from some scratches, they seemed to have survived the fall. Dennis staggered to his feet and then held out his hand to help Gloria up. "Are you okay?" he asked anxiously. She stood still for a while as if trying to make up her mind but eventually said,

"Surprisingly, yes, although I think in the morning I'm going to have bruises in some unusual places."

Dawkins had left the light on. They looked around the room, which seemed to be, part garage and part storage. There were various engine parts and patches of oil on the floor, several shelves covered in tools and cardboard boxes piled against the walls. "Let's look around quickly, and then we better try and get out," Dennis shouted. "He left the light on, so he may be coming back." He opened a cardboard box and looked inside. It just appeared to contain household items.

"What are we looking for?" Gloria asked.

"Anything that looks like A Man from Paris with a Very Large Head," he told her. It soon became apparent that they were not going to find the missing painting in the lock-up, so they turned their attention to trying to get back outside. They looked up and could see the stars in the sky. A sheet of tin was bent down towards them. Dennis had one last look around. "Pity there is no ladder," he said, but Gloria was already dragging a table towards him.

"If I stand on this I may be able to pull myself up onto the roof and then I can pull you up."

Dennis helped her up onto the table. "Be careful, you don't cut yourself on that tin," he warned her. She reached up and bent the tin down further. There was now a good size gap to climb through, but unfortunately, even when she stood on her tiptoes, she couldn't quite reach high enough to pull herself up.

"It's no good; you will have to lift me up on your shoulders, Dennis." He climbed up onto the wobbling table, bent forward and Gloria sat down on the back of his head. "Stand up," she ordered. Dennis was just straining with the effort of lifting her when suddenly they heard the sound of a loud engine getting closer. "Come on, Dennis, quick," she shouted. Dennis strained and strained, the noise from the engine suddenly stopped. He made one last effort, sweat running down his face, and just as the door to the lockup opened, he managed to rise to his full height, with Gloria sitting on his shoulders.

"What's going on, who are you?" an angry voice shouted.

Dennis slowly turned around, with Gloria perched on his shoulders and his legs shaking violently. As he did so, the man removed his helmet and pulled the balaclava off his head, revealing ex-Sergeant Dawkins.

Immediately, Dennis shouted, "Oh, there you are, Mr Dawkins, we have been looking everywhere for you."

Dawkins suddenly realised who it was. "Bisskit, is that you, what are you doing here?"

Dennis looked surprised at the question. "Well, I live in Dudley, so it's not far out of my way."

Dawkins shook his head. "No, I mean what are you doing inside my lock-up, and how did you get in, by the way, considering I locked the door."

Dennis smirked as if it were a stupid question and pointed up towards the hole in the roof. "We came in that way."

Gloria decided it was time she took over; she waved down at the man and said, "Hi, I'm Gloria, let me explain. Dennis and I were out for a drive and he saw you, and said 'Oh, there's Mr Dawkins, I wanted to tell him something' so we turned around and drove after you and saw you walk down here to this lock-up, so we came to see you, but just as we were going to knock on your door I thought I heard a cat on the roof and Dennis wanted to leave it, but I got upset, didn't I Dennis?"

Dennis had no idea what she was talking about, so he just nodded his head. "So, I said we must rescue that cat, and I saw a dustbin by the side of the lock-up, so we climbed up onto the roof and would you believe it when we got up there, the cat had gone." Dawkins looked like he didn't believe a word of it, so she continued. "And then just at that moment, we heard an engine start and Dennis shouted, 'Mr Dawkins!!' very loudly, but you couldn't hear him, and the next second we fell through the roof. We were just trying to get out when, luckily, you returned." Dawkins just stood there, staring up at them. Dennis's legs were aching so he leaned forward and let Gloria hop off his shoulders. They stepped down off the table, and Dennis said, "Anyway, I can see you are very busy, so we will be off," They started to walk towards the door, but all of a sudden Dawkins held his hand up to stop them.

"Just a minute, just a minute, there's something not right here. What did you want to see me about?"

Dennis looked confused. So, Dawkins pointed at Gloria. "She said you followed me because you had something to tell me."

Dennis stared back at him, "Yes, she did, she definitely said that, didn't she? I remember her saying that" then suddenly a smile came to his face, and he reached into his jacket pocket, praying that they would still be there. He pulled something from his pocket and held his hand out towards the security guard. "M.J.K. Smith's lucky bails," he proudly announced, "I forgot to give them to you when I gave you the stumps. Uncle Jimmy said they were always his favourite bails." As soon has Dawkins held them in his hand, he seemed to forget about Dennis and Gloria completely. As they walked passed him, he said, "I've always wanted to get my hands on his bails."

They quickly made their way back to Dennis's car.

"He's a little bit strange," Gloria said.

Dennis looked surprised, "He seems perfectly normal to me."

Chapter 24

The following morning, the lads sat opposite one another in their office and compared notes.

"It was just a complete re-enactment of the previous evening," Stinky explained.

Dennis nodded, "The passionate kiss?"

"Absolutely."

"A room at the hotel?"

"Same room, the same amount of time?"

"Then another passionate kiss when they left the hotel?"

"Even more passionate, if anything."

Dennis stared thoughtfully at the sleeve of his jacket and then removed some egg yolk that had attached itself. "Strange," he said, "I haven't even eaten eggs, someone must have deliberately put an egg on my jacket," He shook his head and tutted as if it were the end of civilisation as we know it. "Anyway, I have to say that Mr Turner's behaviour is very slightly suspicious, but we should not jump to conclusions."

Stinky nodded in agreement. "I agree, I would hate to ruin a man's good name if it turns out to be perfectly innocent."

"Well, that's agreed then," Dennis announced, "We will give it another day or so, just to be certain of our facts."

Stinky topped up their cups from the teapot and asked.

"So, how did your evening go?"

Dennis told him all about their adventures from the previous evening in Dawkins' lock-up. He managed to underplay Gloria's role in their escape greatly, whilst obviously, greatly exaggerating his own importance, but Stinky could not help but notice how his friend's face lit up when proclaiming that, 'for a girl' she had done exceptionally well.

"And?" Stinky asked.

"And what?" Dennis replied.

Stinky sighed. "Details please, for Uncle Stinky. Was there any passionate kissing involved, like Mr Turner and his secretary?"

Dennis looked shocked. "Stinky, please!! A gentleman never kisses and tells, but let's just say that at some point in the evening, our lips may have crossed paths."

Stinky suddenly chuckled. "Has it occurred to you that if you ended up marrying Gloria, you would be Buckethead's son-in-law?"

Dennis put his head in his hands. "What do you mean, has it occurred to me. It occurs to me every time I see her. It's holding me back, Stinky. I like her very much, but I keep imagining what it would be like in the inner sanctum of Planet Plunkett. He would probably have us all down doing push-ups at the wedding reception. It's a nightmare, Stinky, I woke up screaming last night."

To take Dennis's mind off it, Stinky turned back to the subject of the security guard.

"So, what do you make of Dawkins, is he our man?"

"We had a good look around the lock-up. Unfortunately, there was no sign of a Picasso hanging on the wall. I don't know what to make of him, to be honest."

"Well, as far as I can see, he's our only hope," Stinky said. "Let's face it, it would have been easy for him, he could have hidden the painting somewhere and will retrieve it later. How big is The Man from Paris with the Very Large Head, by the way?"

Dennis consulted his notes, "eighteen inches by eighteen inches."

Stinky was amazed, "Is that all? I imagined it was much bigger than that. I mean the man from Paris's head can't be all that large, there isn't enough room for a really large head."

Dennis looked up and explained to his friend. "It's all about proportion, Stinky. I mean I haven't seen the painting but say, for example, the man from Paris's body is an inch high, but his head is another two inches on top of that; well, you can see he would have a very large head in proportion to his body."

Stinky still looked confused, so Dennis explained further.

"Take, for example, if Picasso painted you. Now you are six feet tall, but if he painted your head another 12 feet tall on top of that, you would look really stupid."

Stinky finally seemed to have got it.

"I see, so if Picasso was painting you. You are two feet tall, so if he painted your head another four feet on top of that, you would look even more stupid."

"Oh, very droll, Stinky," Dennis said, "Highly amusing, but you will be pleased to know that when I measured my height the other day, I had grown another quarter of an inch, I am now five feet, five and three quarters of an inch tall, and not only that, my friend, but Gloria said to me yesterday, that I am perfectly proportioned."

Stinky spluttered his mouthful of tea all over the table.

"Perfectly proportioned? How would that even come up in a conversation?"

Dennis thought for a moment.

"Well, we were sitting in the car eating a chocolate digestive, and I said, 'Would you like another one?' and she said, 'I better not, I'd like to be a bit lighter', and I said, 'I'd like to be a bit taller', and she said, 'No, Dennis, you're perfectly proportioned.' So, what do you think of that?"

"What do I think of that?" Stinky asked, "Well, it's not really much of a compliment, is it? She could have said, you are very attractive Dennis, or you are so good-looking, Dennis, but no, the best she could come up with was, you're perfectly proportioned."

Dennis sighed.

"Well it's okay for you, you're six-foot tall, with hair like Mick Jagger. But take it from me, when you are five feet, five and three-quarters of an inch tall, with thinning, ginger hair. Perfectly proportioned is as good as it gets. I was very happy with it."

"Well, in that case I am very pleased for you," Stinky told him, "but here's a word of advice that might come in handy in the future when a girl says to you, 'I'd like to be a bit lighter,' the correct response is, 'No, you're perfect just the way you are,' not, 'I'd like to be a bit taller.'"

"Thank you, Stinky," Dennis replied, 'I will certainly bear that in mind. Meanwhile, I think tonight, seeing as it's Friday, you should pop down to The Red Lion pub in Handsworth and have a quiet drink with Jane Fonda the cleaning lady."

Stinky groaned.

"Oh no, why?"

"Well, she seems to know about everyone who works at the Art Gallery. See what she knows about Dawkins, find out any gossip."

Stinky didn't look happy, so Dennis added.

"Come on; you know you've been dying to see her again."

Part 3

The Scottish man took a bottle and two glasses out of the wardrobe. He half-filled the glasses and then passed one to the other person in the room. "Drink up, Charlie, we can indulge in a small celebration."

He smiled, but it didn't make him look any less scary. Then he looked down at the canvas lying on top of the bed. "I'll tell you what, I wouldn't even hang that in my toilet. Still, if someone is willing to pay me big money, I don't suppose it matters what I think."

The person on the other side of the bed nodded, just wishing to get away as quickly as possible.

The Scottish man slammed down his glass on a bedside table. "What's that face for? We've got away with it. We are just going to carry on as normal until all the fuss dies down, and then we'll be rich. The police are still looking for that West Indian lad you set up. How did you do that by the way, Charlie?"

"It was easy, I just put the word out that he was pilfering, he got the sack, and then I just made sure the police heard about it."

The Scottish man smiled his scary smile again. "Very clever, Charlie. See, we make a great team; you have nothing to worry about."

But Charlie still looked worried. "What about that little ginger bloke, calls himself a Private Investigator, he's still hanging around the Art Gallery, keeps asking questions."

The Scottish man smiled his scariest smile yet. "Don't you worry yourself about Little Ginger, I'll take good care of him "

Chapter 25

The Scottish man turned up the collar of his jacket and walked casually down the street. He'd never set foot in Dudley before, but long ago, he'd learnt that if you move around confidently, at ease in your surroundings, people take no notice of you. It's only when you seem hesitant, that you start to attract attention.

As he walked along, he checked out the street numbers. Not far now.

He quietly hummed a tune. It was a refrain from Beethoven's 8th Symphony, an old favourite. Most people seemed to prefer his 6th Symphony, or of course the 9th. They would probably say that Beethoven's 8th Symphony was too light-hearted, but then the Scottish man was not like other people.

Must be close now, he thought, and then he spotted the car parked by the side of the road. It was a Ford Cortina, and as he drew closer, he noticed that it had seen better days. *Obviously, there isn't much money in Private Investigating*, he thought and allowed himself a smile.

He walked passed it and quickly glanced up at the house. The curtains were closed and all seemed quiet. He looked around him; the street was deserted, so he quickly turned, walked back past the car, turned around again, and this time as he neared the car, he stepped out into the road and passed it on the driver's side. One last glance around and then he dropped to the floor and rolled underneath the car.

It happened so quickly that if someone had been looking down the street, they would have thought they must have imagined it.

He just lay there for a few seconds, then he reached inside his jacket and removed the hacksaw blade. It was wrapped in a small piece of cloth. He reached up and wiped the brake line, and then commenced sawing. After a few seconds, he stopped humming Beethoven's 8th and, using his feet and elbows, pushed himself away from under the line. Then he reached across and sawed a bit more. Suddenly, liquid started to appear and drip to the ground. He placed the cloth and hacksaw back inside his jacket and was just about to roll from under the car when he heard a door open. He glanced back towards the house and shook his head. A young ginger-haired man was standing in the doorway, checking something in an old briefcase. The Scottish man hated mistakes. He'd been told that the Private Investigator never left for work before eight am, he glanced at his watch, it was only seven-fifteen. "This isn't good enough," he muttered. Then, he noticed the man had turned back to close the front door, so he quickly rolled out from under the car, leapt to his feet, straightened his jacket and commenced walking down the road.

Dennis had decided to go to work early that morning. He couldn't sleep so he thought he might as well grab a cup of tea in town and drink it in peace before heading to the office, rather than sit and have breakfast with his parents and have them ask him when he was going to get a proper job.

As he turned from the door, he noticed a well-built man with short, greying hair walking past his car. He seemed to have appeared from nowhere.

Dennis ran the engine for a couple of minutes and slowly moved off down the road. Just before he turned left to head into the town centre, he passed the man; he appeared to be humming a tune but glanced over when he heard the car and nodded. Dennis had never seen the man before but nodded back and waved, because his mother had always told him, "Politeness doesn't cost you anything".

Chapter 26

"*It was so good of you to pick me up from the hospital Shirley,*" Gladys told the lady driving the car. "*I just don't know how I would have managed without you lately.*"

"*Nonsense, Gladys,*" she replied, "*What are neighbours for. I'm pleased to help, you've been through a very traumatic experience. I can't imagine what it must have been like suddenly having Miss Plunge appear in your garden like that.*"

Gladys Bouvier was quiet for several minutes, and then, as they turned up Arcadia Avenue, she said in a quiet voice. "It's not so much Miss Plunge. At least she has finally been laid to rest. No, it's that little ginger-haired chap I still see in my nightmares. I don't think I will ever forget the look of sheer terror on his face that day as Miss Plunge landed on top of him, staring at him, with her one eye."

Shirley took one hand off the steering wheel and patted Gladys on her leg. "Now, now, that's all in the past, you need to put it all behind you. I'm sure the little ginger-haired chap has done just that"

The little ginger-haired chap in question was, at that very moment, leaving a café and getting back into his car. He pulled away from the kerb, failing to notice the pool of oil lying on the road, where he'd been parked. It was still quiet on the roads as he turned right and made his way down a big hill. Halfway down the hill, he touched the brake to slow his descent down a bit and was surprised to see that nothing happened. He pushed the brake all the way down to the floor but felt nothing. Dennis was always a very careful driver, he was one of the few people he knew that actually wore their seatbelt and always drove below the speed limit. Stinky was always telling him to speed up a bit, and now he found himself travelling faster and faster. He stood and jumped up and down on the brake pedal, but it was to no avail.

At the bottom of the hill he knew he would hit the main road, he prayed that there were no cars coming. As he shot past the stop sign, he thought he had never travelled this fast in his life. He closed his eyes and flew across the main road, neither breathing nor seeing the look of horror on the face of the driver of the car he just missed. When he reopened his eyes, he had crossed the main road and was now hurtling up the hill opposite. At least this time he was heading uphill. He suddenly recognised that he was on Arcadia Avenue. Only a few days ago he had been sitting on top of a coffin flying down the hill in the opposite direction. The car gradually started to slow down with the effort of travelling up the steep hill. Maybe I have a chance, Dennis thought.

"Are you sure you will be okay, Gladys?" Shirley asked her neighbour.

"Yes, I'll be fine now I'm home. I'm just going to get the washing in, and then I'll make us a nice cup of tea. You just sit over there."

As Dennis reached halfway up the hill, there was a car parked in front of a house, so he pulled out towards the centre of the road to go around it. But unfortunately, a large furniture removal van chose that exact moment to come down the hill. Dennis realised the van would pass the parked car at the same moment as he would reach it. He had a split second to decide and then realised he had no choice. At the last moment, rather than smash head-on into the van or the parked car, he turned left, up onto the pavement. He spotted a small wall in front of him; it appeared to be damaged from a previous accident. His last thought as the car hit the wall was; I've been here before.

Gladys removed the drying from the clothesline and then had a good look around. She would have to get someone in to fix that front wall, and there was still some damage to the lawn. Still, it was good to be home. She bent down to smell her roses, and at that second heard a deafening crash.

The car had slowed down a considerable amount by now but still hit the wall at such speed that when it came to a sudden stop, the back of the car rose, and for a second, Dennis balanced on top of the wall on the front wheels. Just long enough for him to wave to a lady who had fallen into some rose bushes, she looked vaguely familiar. Then the car slowly toppled over onto its roof.

121

On hearing the terrible sound, Gladys looked up, screamed and fell into the rose bushes. In front of her was a terrifying sight. A car rose onto its front wheels and balanced on her wall. Someone inside waved to her, she spotted ginger hair, and then she fainted.

Chapter 27

Stinky couldn't believe it. "The same house? That's amazing. How's Mrs Bouvier?"

Dennis shook his head, "I'm afraid it's not looking good, they had to put her into a straitjacket. She just kept screaming, "He's back, he's back.""

Stinky poured his friend a cup of tea, "It's amazing you survived Ginge."

"We'll let this be a lesson to you, Stinky, always wear the seatbelt. The policeman said I would have been seriously hurt or worse if I hadn't."

Stinky nodded, "What about the car, has it survived your bad driving?"

"Well, it's still lying on its roof in Mrs Bouvier's front garden at the moment. One thing I did notice though, whilst it was upside down is that the accident had nothing to do with me driving badly. Someone had deliberately cut through the brakes."

Stinky spat his tea out all over the office table.

"Oh, come on, Ginge, are you sure?"

"Of course, I'm sure, and the police constable who turned up confirmed it. He said it looked like it was cut with a hacksaw blade."

Stinky still found it hard to believe.

"Could it not have been an accident?"

Dennis sipped his tea and considered the question.

"Well, I suppose if someone was walking down the road with a hacksaw blade in their hand, and as they passed my car, they slipped over onto their backs, slid under the car and accidentally sawed through my brake line, as they slid past it. That is a possibility, but in all honesty, Stinky, I somehow doubt that is what happened. So, the next question is who did it, who have I upset enough that they would try and kill me?"

"It is strange," Stinky said, "because you are often referred to as The Most Popular Man in Dudley."

Dennis sighed, "Now I know you are being sarcastic, Stinky, which as I've told you many times is the lowest form of wit, but it is true, as far as I know, I have made few enemies, certainly none that wish me to join Miss Plunge in the Cemetery, so I can only conclude it is someone I have just recently upset, and I'm guessing it's something to do with the Man from Paris with the Very Large Head."

Stinky gasped, "Do you think it's Dawkins?"

"I'm not sure whether he's involved or not, but I think I saw the man who did it." Dennis went on to tell his friend about the man he'd seen lurking near his car.

"When I drove past him, he looked up and nodded," Dennis told him, "and I'll tell you something, Stinky. He smiled at me, and I remember thinking, it wasn't a very pleasant smile."

His friend still seemed a bit shaken, so Stinky tried to cheer him up.

"Well, if you think you've had a scary morning, you should have been with me in The Red Lion last night, I thought I wouldn't get out alive. There was Jean, the cleaning lady, and her best friend, Beryl."

"Did she look like Jane Fonda as well?" Dennis asked.

"They looked like twins," Stinky replied, "The Gruesome Twosome. Every time I asked a question, it cost me a drink and a cuddle. It got even worse later; I had to dance with them and join in a rendition of Roll out the Barrel. Believe me Ginge; I would much have preferred to be hurtling downhill in a car with no brakes."

At last, Dennis laughed.

"Well, was it all just fun and games or did you actually find out anything useful?" he asked.

"Nothing that really helps," Stinky replied. "She reckons that Dawkins is too boring to get involved in anything illegal. She said his only secret passion is his motorcycle, he spends all his spare time polishing it, or riding around pretending he's Marlon Brando in the Wild One."

Dennis rubbed his eyes.

"So, looks like we are back to square one." Stinky continued.

"Oh, I don't think so," Dennis said. "We just don't realise yet what it is we have discovered. But whatever it is, it's worried someone enough to want to kill me. We just need to find out what it is, that we know."

As usual, Dennis had managed to confuse him. So, Stinky changed the subject.

"Don't forget that you are coming around for tea tonight, and Gloria is invited."

Dennis pulled a face.

"Do I really have to, you know I'm not very good at that sort of thing, plus I'm worried that Brenda will make her stew and dumplings again. M.J.K. Smith could have used those dumplings as cricket balls; I had to go to the dentist the last time, I damaged two teeth on them."

Stinky laughed.

"Yes, you do, I can't keep making excuses. Anyway, I need you to convince Brenda that being Private Investigators is a proper job and that one day soon, we will start making some money out of it."

Dennis sulked, but finally said,

"Okay, I'll call Gloria, but I'm warning you, the first sign of a dumpling and I'm out of there."

Chapter 28

Brenda placed the steaming plate of stew on the table in front of Dennis. "Look what's on top," she said, smiling down at him. "My special dumplings. I nearly forgot, and then Jack told me they were your favourite."

"Brilliant," Dennis replied, "it's just lucky, that he remembered me telling him."

He glanced over at Stinky, but he appeared to be busy with a fingernail, so instead he turned and looked at Gloria, who he could tell was trying not to laugh. As they had driven to the house, he had told her all about his aversion to Brenda's dumplings.

As Brenda walked back to the kitchen, Dennis tapped one of the dumplings with his spoon and grimaced when it made a clanging noise.

"I'd watch your teeth on those," Stinky mumbled helpfully, and then before his friend could reply, he asked Gloria if she had heard from her father lately.

"He's a wonderful man," he added, "We do hope he's enjoying himself in Berlin."

Gloria laughed. "You don't have to pretend," she said, "I know how you soldiers felt about him, do you know some of them used to call him Buckethead behind his back?"

Dennis tried to look shocked.

"No, surely not. I find that very hard to believe. Well, I can tell you now that Stinky and I always had the utmost respect for him." Stinky nodded in agreement.

Gloria looked surprised. "Really, because I must say, he said some very harsh things about you, Dennis, especially that day when I first took you back to our house. He used language that day that I'd never heard before or since. I thought he was going to have a heart attack."

"Probably just overcome with emotion," Dennis said.

"Yes, that would be it," Stinky added. "He was just so happy to see his favourite soldier at the centre of Planet Plunkett."

They all laughed, even Brenda who had now joined them and was trying to spoon more dumplings onto Dennis's plate.

"How come you left the army, Jack?" Gloria asked. "Dennis told me you could have been a Sergeant by now.

Everyone went quiet until Stinky said. "Oh, I suppose I'd had enough, I had got a bit sick of army life."

Dennis didn't say anything; he knew that his friend had loved army life more than anything and had been ready to sign on for another few years. But once he had heard that there was a two-year posting to Germany coming up, he had known he would have to leave. Brenda loved Dudley. Her family lived nearby, and he had known immediately that there was no way she would consider moving to another country. He had left the army for Brenda. Dennis always felt a bit guilty about it, because, when Stinky had told him that he too would be leaving the army, his first thought was one of joy that his friend would still be by his side. Stinky was at such a loss about what to do with his future; it had been easy to talk him into joining Dennis in his new Private Investigator business.

"I hear your car is out of action for a few days," Brenda suddenly said.

They had decided not to mention the cut brake-line so as not to worry the girls.

"Yes, nothing much, just a little accident," Dennis said.

"That's not what Jack said." Brenda continued, "He said it was due to your atrocious driving skills."

Dennis looked over at his friend, "Oh is it, is that what Jack said, well I think Jack may be forgetting that a small dog ran in front of me, and I decided to sacrifice myself in order to save that dog because that's the sort of wonderful person I am. Is that not right, Jack?"

Stinky was busy hiding a dumpling in a vase of flowers, whilst everyone was looking at Dennis.

He quickly looked up, and said, "Oh yes, that's right, it all comes back to me now."

"Anyway," Dennis added. "I'll certainly be glad when I get it back from the garage. I've borrowed Granddad's old car, and it would be quicker to walk."

He suddenly changed the subject

"Is that a new ornament?" he asked, pointing towards a shelf on the far wall. When everyone turned to look, he quickly rolled a dumpling behind the sofa.

Brenda shook her head. "Of course not, it's always been there. Men just don't notice things, do they, Gloria?" Gloria nodded in agreement and the next ten minutes was taken up with criticising men's inability to listen, notice things, and shop.

"Jack's hopeless, I can tell him something, and five minutes later he's forgotten it."

"I asked Dennis which colour top would go best with this skirt, and he said army green."

Brenda gasped as if this was the most outrageous thing she had ever heard.

The lads looked at one another and kept quiet. They already knew that it was best to stay clear of these sorts of conversations.

Gloria suddenly noticed some framed photographs on a shelf. They were obviously of Stinky and Brenda's wedding. Brenda was wearing a lovely wedding dress, whilst Stinky and Dennis looked rather dashing in their army uniforms. The next photo was of the reception. People of all ages, sitting around with their glasses raised. Next, to the seated Brenda and Stinky, a man she didn't recognise appeared to be making a speech. She could see no sign of Dennis.

Brenda realised what it was Gloria was looking at and said.

"That's Billy, Billy Flynn. An old friend of Jack's. He kindly stepped in to make the Best Man's speech."

She noticed that Gloria looked a bit confused.

"Because of what happened to Dennis."

Gloria looked even more confused, and then it dawned on Brenda

"He hasn't told you?" she asked, "He hasn't told you what happened at the wedding?"

Dennis tried to change the subject and then said that he couldn't really remember the details. But everyone insisted that he must tell Gloria the story. Eventually, Dennis gave in and poured himself a glass of beer from the big bottle Stinky had placed on the table.

"I'm going to need a drink," he mumbled. He glanced at Gloria and then across at his best friend and Brenda. They had big smiles on their faces because they knew what was coming.

"It's not really one-story, Gloria, it's two stories, and the first one started about ten years ago when Stinky…erm, I mean Jack and I were about 14. School holidays were coming up. We were wondering what to do, and then out of the blue, Jack received a letter from his Uncle Norman."

Dennis took another sip of beer, sighed loudly and then let his mind drift back to..

SUMMER 1959, THE COPPER KETTLE CAFÉ, IN DUDLEY

Stinky had started to tell Dennis about his father's brother, Uncle Norman. But Dennis was more intrigued by the mention of his friend's father. All he knew was that Stinky's dad had disappeared without a trace many years ago and Stinky didn't like to talk about him. "I'm not one to pry," Dennis interrupted him, "But we've been friends for a long time now, I think it's time you told me what happened to your dad."

Stinky was quiet for a moment and then said, "Well, there's not much to tell, he disappeared when I was about six, all I know is that Mum sent him out to get some potatoes for tea and he never came back."

Dennis felt sad for his friend and said, "That's terrible, what did your mum do?"

Stinky thought for a while, and then replied, "Well, it was a long time ago, but I seem to recall she did beans on toast."

"No!! Not for tea, I mean what did she do about your dad going missing?" Dennis asked, "Did the police search for him?"

"Oh, I see," said his friend. "Well, I don't think she did much for a few days, they weren't that close from what I remember, she used to shout at him a lot. Eventually, she mentioned it to the police, but nothing came of it. She waited over the weekend and then rented the spare room out. She said she needed someone to carry the coal in and that's all Dad had been handy for. I remember asking about him once, and she said that a lot of men came back from the war and they had changed but unfortunately, he hadn't, he was useless before he went and he was useless when he came back."

Dennis was shocked. "That's not very nice," he said, "Has she never wanted to remarry?"

Now it was Stinky's turn to look shocked. "You've met my mother Ginge, would you want to marry her?"

"Well she's a bit old for me," he replied, "I'm not even fourteen yet, but I see what you mean, she is a bit scary, and don't forget, I have tasted her cooking."

They both grimaced at the thought. "I remember it well," Stinky exclaimed, "You were stuck on our toilet for several days after that Shepherd's Pie, me and Mum had to use next doors' toilet, it was quite inconvenient."

"Well, I'm sorry," Dennis told him, "It was fairly inconvenient for me, I couldn't move for days. I tried once, but it was a disaster, those were my favourite trousers as well. No, I couldn't marry someone who couldn't cook, what would be the point?"

Stinky nodded in agreement and said, "You're lucky Dennis, your mum makes great cakes and apple pies."

"Exactly," his friend replied, "I'm just going to live with my mum forever. Anyway, enough of that, now you know I like a good mystery Stinky, were there no clues as to what happened to your dad?"

His friend shook his head and then said, "No, it was a complete mystery. The only really strange thing was that Mrs Talbert, who worked at the pub that Dad used to drink in, also disappeared at the same time."

Dennis stared into space for a while, then smiled and shook his head, "Stinky, my old friend, you are so naïve, don't you see what's happened here?" Stinky looked bewildered, so Dennis continued, "Just think about it, I've lived in Dudley all my life, and I've never heard of anyone disappearing, and yet a man and a woman disappeared on the same night. I do realise that I'm more intellectual than the average person, but it's fairly obvious to me what went on here." Stinky still look bewildered, so Dennis explained it simply, "Alien abduction, I've read about this sort of thing, but this is the first conclusive proof I've ever had. There's no way I can break this gently to you Stinky, but

I'm afraid there is a very good chance that your father and Mrs Talbert are living on another planet."

Stinky shook his head, "I can't believe that I've never considered that before, it all makes sense, but why would intelligent beings from another planet want my father, if he was as useless as Mum says he was?"

"Well, of course, they wouldn't have known that when they abducted him," Dennis replied, "maybe they just needed someone to get the coal in, anyway now we've solved that mystery, tell me about Uncle Norman."

***

Stinky suddenly interrupted his friend's reminiscing.

"I'd forgotten about you saying Dad had been abducted by aliens, Ginge. As you well know, a few months back, using my new-found detective skills, I was able to locate my long-lost father. He was living in Yorkshire with a certain Mrs Marjorie Talbert. So, for once, the great detective Dennis Bisskit got it wrong, they weren't abducted by aliens at all."

Dennis thought for a moment and before replying.

"Well, to be fair, I was half right, I did say they would be living on another planet, and you found them in Yorkshire."

Stinky laughed and said, "Good point." But Gloria suddenly said.

"Well that is all very interesting, but what does it have to do with you missing Brenda and Jack's wedding reception?"

Dennis leaned back and let his mind return to summer, 1959.

***

Stinky explained to his friend that his missing father's brother, Uncle Norman owned a farm in Colwall, near the Malvern Hills. "I've never heard you mention this Uncle Norman before," Dennis told him.

"Well I haven't really given him much thought," Stinky explained. "I've only met him once. We visited the farm before Dad was abducted by aliens, I was about six, but he's never been mentioned since. I think he's the black sheep of the family."

Dennis was surprised. "I thought you were the black sheep of the family," he said.

"Oh no," his friend replied, "I'm just the grey sheep of the family, I don't think there's anything actually wrong with Uncle Norman, he's just a bit eccentric."

"Oh well, there you go then, that would explain everything," Dennis said, "It's been my experience that the vast majority of people who are called eccentric are in fact stark raving bonkers."

"I've heard you referred to as eccentric," Stinky told him, but Dennis quickly explained. "Yes, but I'm one of those few eccentric people who are actually eccentric. Anyway, tell me about this farm."

"It's just a farm," Stinky said, "You know, sheep, cows, chickens, ducks, that sort of thing, it's called Green Grass Farm, Uncle Norman lives on his own, the man who works for him is away for a few weeks, and Uncle Norman sent me a letter, asking if I wanted to come and help out during the holidays, he said I could bring a friend, and he'd pay us."

It sounded good, but Dennis hesitated, he knew there must be a catch somewhere. "What sort of work and how much pay?" he asked.

Stinky smiled and replied, "He didn't say, but come on Ginge, it's a paid holiday, it's a lovely spot, all hills and rivers, we can go fishing and hiking."

"Dennis was quiet for a few minutes and then made up his mind, "Right, let's do it, my friend, let's be farmers for a couple of weeks, but it all sounds too good to be true, and if there are any disasters I shall hold you personally responsible." Stinky nodded in agreement although he knew for a fact that wherever Dennis went, there were disasters, and he didn't really see why he should be held responsible.

***

Dennis suddenly turned to face Gloria, before continuing.

"Now, what you need to understand about Uncle Norman was that he was madly in love with Blanch Gibblet. She had worked for him for years, cooking and cleaning. Jack and I realised straight away that they were in love with each other, but neither seemed to be able to do anything about it. Blanch kept dropping hints, but Uncle Norman was very shy. He had a bad stutter which made it difficult. It all came to a head one morning. We were waiting for Blanch to bring in the breakfast tray."

***

They were sat at the big wooden table, waiting for Blanche to appear. Uncle Norman followed them in, but just as he was about to sit down, he noticed that his bootlace had come undone, he knelt on one knee to retie it, just at that moment Blanche had entered the room carrying a tray. She looked stunned when she spotted him down on one knee and even more so when he opened his mouth and said, "B..B.Blanche, will you ma..ma." Blanche looked like she might faint. "W..Will you ma..ma." Dennis grabbed hold of Stinky's arm, "W..Will you ma..ma..manage, to clean the barn tomorrow?" Blanche looked like she might burst into tears, she dropped the tray onto the table and walked back into the kitchen slamming the door behind her. "I'll never understand wer..women," Uncle Norman said, but the lads were busy tucking into the cake.

***

"Typical man," Brenda shouted. Gloria nodded in agreement.

Dennis topped up his drink again and said, "The next part of the tale is still a bit traumatic for me, so no interruptions please."

***

The next morning, there was a very bad atmosphere. Blanch suddenly said she would be leaving early to get ready for the big, annual, Colwall Barn Dance. Evidently, it's the social event of the year. Anyway, the shock was, Blanche said that Walter Watkins had asked her to accompany him. Uncle Norman couldn't believe it.

"W..W.Walter W..Watkins," he'd stammered, "but he's only got one ear, he, ler..ler….lost the other in the w..war."

Blanche just glared back at him and replied.

"Well, he might only have one ear, but at least he listens to me with it."

Later, Uncle Norman came up with a plan. He would pay us to go to the Barn Dance, keep an eye on Blanch and Walter Watkins, and then report back to him.

***

Gloria suddenly took one of Dennis's hands in her own, feeling that they were approaching the traumatic part of the tale.

***

That evening at seven pm, Uncle Norman dropped them off near the old building where the Barn Dance was being held. "Now remember ler..lads, don't take your eyes off Ber..Blanche and Walter Watkins." The boys didn't move; they just stared at him.

"We are going to need money for a snack," Stinky said, and eventually, reluctantly, Uncle Norman reached into his jacket pocket, pulled out a coin, and handed it to Stinky. "We are both going to need a snack," Dennis told him, and even more reluctantly, he produced another coin and gave it to Dennis. "Spend that wer..wisely, lads," he said. The boys jumped down from the truck and made their way to the building; there was already a bit of a queue outside. The lads had made little effort to smarten themselves up, but it was obvious that for some this was the social event of the year. Most of the ladies wore long, floral dresses and some of the men had even polished their Wellington Boots. When they finally made it inside, they saw a stage set up at one end of the room. All the chairs were pushed against the walls, leaving a large dance area. At the far end of the room were a couple of tables, one holding sandwiches and cakes, and the other selling drinks. "See," Stinky shouted, "I don't know why you were worried, this looks great."

Dennis didn't look convinced, "We shall see," he muttered. They went and got a glass of lemonade and a piece of fruit cake and then found a couple of chairs at the back of the room so that they could keep an eye on the door.

"No sign of Blanche yet," Stinky said.

Dennis looked around the room and replied, "Maybe she made it all up about Walter Watkins asking her out just to make Norman jealous." They relaxed and enjoyed their refreshments, then a couple of men climbed on stage, one with an accordion and the other with a violin. They started quietly tuning up. Another man joined them and tried to speak into the microphone. It made a loud whistling noise, making everyone put their hands over their ears. The man apologised and made some adjustments, then he tapped the microphone several times with his finger, before speaking into it, "Testing, testing, one two, one, two, Good evening, ladies and gentlemen, and welcome to tonight's event, I hope you are all in a dancing mood, I expect to see everyone up on the dance floor." Dennis immediately slid down into his seat, hoping to make himself invisible. The announcer continued, "We are very lucky tonight," he turned and pointed at the two men tuning their instruments, "We have for your entertainment, possibly the finest accordion player in Herefordshire, Rodney 'The Maestro' Dingwell, and the George Formby of the fiddle, Bert Bummington." The crowd applauded enthusiastically, and the musicians gave a quick wave.

There was quite a good crowd in by now, but still no sign of Blanche. Dennis stood up and said, "I'm off to the toilet, guard my chair."

Just after he'd left, the announcer said. "Ladies and Gentlemen, choose your partners for the first dance." People suddenly moved in all directions, grabbing a dance partner and then making their way to the dance floor.

Suddenly, Stinky spotted the biggest person he'd ever seen striding towards him. As they got closer, he realised it was a woman, wearing a large cowboy hat, a checked shirt and jeans tucked into green Wellington Boots. Stinky's next-door neighbour was the largest coal miner in Dudley, he had arms bigger than Stinky's legs, but he was smaller than this lady. She stopped in front of Stinky and grunted, "Dance!!" He immediately fell to the ground clutching his knee, "I'd love to," he said, "but it's the old knee injury, the doctor said I have to rest." Then, out of the corner of his eye, he spotted Dennis heading his way; he nodded towards him and added, "My friend, Dennis was just saying he would love a dance." She didn't even bother asking Dennis, she just lifted him up under one arm and carried him to the dance floor. He glanced back at Stinky with a terrified expression on his face, but Stinky quickly looked away and fiddled with his shoelace, pretending he hadn't noticed. When he looked back, everyone was in a large circle. The large lady cowboy/coal miner had Dennis by the right hand, and he wasn't going anywhere. The music started and the announcer commenced shouting instructions. "Swing to the right, swing to the left." Dennis, who was in shock, kept swinging to the right when he should have been swinging to the left, but luckily the lady, cowboy/coal miner would wrench him back in the opposite direction, nearly tearing his arm from its socket every time she did it. At one stage, she improvised, picked Dennis up and threw him into the air, nearly banging his head on the ceiling. She shouted "Yippee!!" as she caught him and twirled him around like a spinning top. Eventually the music stopped, Dennis staggered back towards Stinky, the blood had drained from his face. "Well, that looked fun," Stinky said. Dennis just stared at him and then said, "No, not fun Stinky, I'm surprised you would think it was fun, I would have thought, the fact that I was crying and screaming would have given you a clue that I wasn't having fun." Stinky tried his best but, eventually, couldn't hold back any longer and started laughing until tears ran down his face, but Dennis wasn't seeing the funny side yet. "It's not funny, Stinky," he said, "She was the scariest person I've ever seen, I'll probably have nightmares for the rest of my life. Why did she want to dance with me?"

"Well she was going to ask me," Stinky replied, "but then she spotted you, with your good looks and charisma, and I was just cast aside."

Dennis suspected there was more to it. He wiped the sweat from his brow and said, "She reminded me of someone in that cowboy movie we watched last month." Stinky thought for a moment and said, "Annie Oakley?" "No," Dennis replied, "Champion the Wonder Horse," but before they could say anything else, Blanche Giblett and Walter Watkins entered the building.

Blanche was wearing a long green dress, covered in white flowers. It looked like she had done something strange to her hair, but Dennis couldn't quite make out what it was. Walter was in his best suit and trilby; it looked like he had bought the suit when he was a much thinner man. He had managed to do up one button, but it was struggling to hold things together. He wore thick glasses, and Dennis was just wondering what held them up on his ear-less side when he turned, and Dennis could see he had a piece of elastic attached to his glasses and running behind his head. He also noticed that every time someone spoke to him, he would turn his good ear towards them. At one point, he was in conversation with a couple who stood either side of him, and it looked like he was watching the tennis, his head kept flying from side to side. The lads kept a low profile for a while, just keeping an eye on things, but then Dennis noticed the large lady cowboy/coal miner staring at him from across the room. She gave a little wave and smiled, well at least Dennis thought she was smiling. It was hard to tell. It looked like she had just read an article about smiling in a magazine and was attempting it for the first time, she wasn't quite getting the hang of it. "Looks like you've made a friend there, Ginge," Stinky said. "If she walks towards me, I'm going to faint," Dennis replied.

Stinky laughed, "You better make it look good, I think she will be able to tell you're acting."

"No," Dennis told him, "I won't be acting, I mean if she walks towards me, I'm literally going to faint, she scares me that much." At that point, as he glanced over at her, she waved again. "I'm going to say hello to Blanche," he said and disappeared before Stinky could reply. Blanche looked surprised to see him and then looked up, smiled and waved at Stinky, before walking across to him with Dennis. "Didn't expect to see you, lads, here," she said, and then had a sudden thought, "Don't tell me Norman sent you to keep an eye on me."

The boys tried to look shocked, "No way," Stinky said, "We just thought it would be a fun evening and, of course, Dennis loves dancing, he's already been up there showing what he can do."

Blanche looked surprised. "Well, I didn't realise you were keen on dancing, I hope you'll have a dance with me later."

Dennis quickly changed the subject. "How are things going with you and Walter, Blanche?" she pulled a face.

"Oh, he's okay, he drives me mad though, keeps wanting to do things for me, I'm quite capable of doing things for myself. Anyway, I better get back to him, they are just about to have a square dance. See you later, boys." Dennis didn't like the sound of a square dance; he was still getting over the effects of the circular dance, so he decided to go and hide in the toilet for a while until it was over. He was just in time as well; seconds after he'd left, Stinky looked up and there right in front of him was the large lady cowboy/coal miner, he immediately fell to the ground again, clutching his leg. She didn't seem surprised.

"Where's yer little friend?" she grunted, as though English wasn't her first language.

"He had to pop out," Stinky stammered, "But he said to tell you to be sure to save the last dance for him."

She stared at him for a moment, then reached down, and with one hand, lifted him up and sat him down on a chair. "I'll be waiting," she grunted, turned and strode off.

When Dennis returned, Stinky felt it was best not to mention this conversation, so instead said, "I wonder why Blanche isn't keen on Walter Watkins, he sounds like a nice man, does stuff for her, women are very strange, Ginge."

"He's maybe too nice," Dennis answered, "she might prefer the bad boy like Uncle Norman. It was the same with Humphrey Bogart; I heard the next-door neighbour tell my mum that she liked Humphrey Bogart because he was a bad boy."

Stinky just stared into space not saying a word, until eventually, Dennis asked him if he was okay. "Yes, I'm fine." he answered, "I've just never heard Uncle Norman, and Humphrey Bogart mentioned in the same sentence before."

Dennis spent the next hour keeping one eye on Blanche and Walter Watkins and the other on the lady cowboy/coal miner who, on a couple of occasions, spotted him looking in her direction and attempted to smile back at him. She still hadn't gotten the hang of it. To avoid her, he wondered over to chat with Blanche again.

"You seem to have made an impression on Lady Gertie," she told him.

Dennis didn't have a clue what she was talking about, so she pointed across the dance floor and said.

"Lady Gertrude Smyth-Fawcett, the Earl of Hereford's daughter."

Dennis couldn't believe it.

"You mean that big, mad woman, in the cowboy hat?"

Blanche chuckled.

"She's not mad, just a little eccentric, that's all."

Stinky was sitting daydreaming when, suddenly, he felt a tap on his shoulder, well not so much a tap, as the feeling of getting hit with a lump of wood. He grabbed his shoulder and turned, horrified to see the big, lady cowboy/coalminer staring down at him.

"It's the last dance, where is he?"

Luckily, out of the corner of his eye, he spotted Dennis walking back towards him.

Stinky quickly nodded in his direction and said.

"Here he is now, and he looks excited."

She knocked several people over has she carried him onto the dance floor.

Half an hour later, the lads slowly made their way along a moonlit track, back towards the farm.

"Well, the good news is," Stinky shouted, "I saw Blanche and Walter Watkins having an argument, she didn't look very happy with him, that should cheer Uncle Norman up."

But Dennis didn't seem interested.

"Stark, raving bonkers. I wouldn't mind, but she can't even dance, she just makes it up as she goes along. I know very little about dancing, Stinky, but I'm fairly certain that you are not supposed to pick your partner up by the ankles and swing them around and around, knocking over other dancers."

Stinky felt that it was best not to get involved in the conversation. Dennis just stared at him and then continued.

"I don't know where she got the idea from that I'd asked her to save the last dance for me, and I notice, no one tried to help me."

"I think everyone was a bit scared," Stinky finally said, "when the announcer asked her to calm down, she threw a chair at him."

"I'm quite aware of what she did," Dennis shouted. "I was sitting on her shoulders at the time, so I had an excellent view."

***

139

He was so engrossed in his memories that Dennis was shocked to realise that everyone was rolling around laughing. Gloria had tears rolling down her cheeks.

"It's not funny," he told them. "I still have nightmares."

Gloria used a handkerchief to wipe her eyes and said.

"So, what happened to Blanche and Uncle Norman?"

Dennis smiled.

"Thanks to Stinky and me, I mean Jack, doing such excellent work, I can report that they got married a few months later and as far as I know, lived happily ever after."

Gloria clapped her hands and said.

"Well done, and Lady Gertie, did you see her again?"

Dennis slowly shook his head.

"Not in Colwall," but Stinky interrupted him.

"Well, you did actually, just for a second. We had to walk into town the next day," he told them.

"Dennis wore Uncle Norman's greatcoat, with the collar turned up to disguise himself. We were just on the edge of town, walking past a big hedgerow when we heard her unmistakable screeching. I turned around, and Dennis had disappeared, he jumped over the fence, not realising that there was a huge drop on the other side, down to the bypass road, he landed on top of a car bonnet."

Dennis nodded.

"Yes, I'd forgotten about that. I landed on Bert and Dorothy, lovely couple. Still, send me Christmas cards."

Stinky ignored the interruption.

"Anyway, I had to come up with some story about Dennis having to rush back to Dudley because his mum was sick. She was most disappointed, said that Dennis was quite possibly the finest dancer of his generation."

Gloria finally stopped laughing and said.

"That was a great story, Dennis, but I still don't see what that has to do with Brenda and Jack's wedding."

Dennis rubbed his eyes, thinking about the Barn dance had worn him out.

"Well, that's why we come to the second story," he mumbled, "but before I tell that I need a cup of tea and cake break."

Brenda and Gloria went into the kitchen and ten minutes later returned with a tray. Whilst Gloria poured cups of tea, Brenda disappeared into another room and came back with a long woollen scarf which she proceeded to wrap around Dennis's neck.

"If you are going to tell the wedding story, you are going to need to keep warm," she said, with a big smile on her face.

Dennis frowned.

"It's not funny Brenda; it's really not funny. What you all need to understand is the terrible effect that evening at the Barn dance had on me. I had nightmares for years afterwards. I kept seeing Lady Gertie striding towards me in my dreams. Then over the years, I gradually started to forget her, although, I thought I spotted her once when I was watching the wrestling. Jackie Pallo was fighting some other bloke."

Gloria interrupted him, "And you thought you spotted her in the audience."

Dennis shook his head.

"Not in the audience. In the ring. She was the spitting image of the man, Jackie Pallo was wrestling, they could have been twins, although obviously, she was a lot bigger. Anyway, eventually, I forgot all about her. Until Brenda had to go and choose that time and place to hold her wedding reception."

***

His mind drifted back to the wedding of Brenda Rumble and Stinky Blackshaw. They had decided to get married on Stinky's next leave from the army; the church was available, but unfortunately, the place where they wanted to hold the reception was fully booked. Eventually, they managed to book the Mount Hotel, just outside Wolverhampton. The wedding went off without a hitch, Brenda dressed in white, and the lads resplendent in their best army uniforms. Apart from one ten minute hold-up, whilst Dennis searched for the rings. They had somehow got stuck in the lining of his uniform jacket but eventually, were retrieved, much to everyone's relief. After the wedding ceremony finished, Dennis witnessed documents being signed, joined in for some photographs and then had to rush off to the Mount Hotel to be able to welcome guests as they arrived. He was accompanied by an old friend of the lads, Billy Flynn. They had known him since their Boy Scouts days, and he'd offered to help in any way he could.

They were first to arrive, they grabbed a quick drink and then waited out the front of the hotel, has guests began to turn up. Billy did most of the meeting and greeting as Dennis sat on a concrete step by the side of the hotel, practising his Best-Man speech. Much as there was never any doubt about Stinky inviting Dennis to be his Best-Man, the speech was his biggest concern. Knowing his friend as he did, he knew that Dennis loved nothing more than making a speech. They generally dragged on and on and were more about Dennis than whatever it was that he was actually talking about. Stinky's fears had been confirmed when he'd noticed his friend carrying a manuscript, the size of a large encyclopaedia, with SPEECH printed on it, a few days earlier.

Guests' cars began to arrive. Well-dressed men, women and children disembarked, and Billy gave them directions.

The Mount Hotel is a distinguished Edwardian building, boasting not only accommodation but several beautiful large rooms, ideal for holding wedding receptions and meetings.

Billy suddenly ran over and shouted for help.

"I can't manage on my own, Dennis," he explained. "There's another wedding going on in the Great Hall, Lord and Lady somebody; I'm getting guests mixed up."

The Great Hall was the biggest and most spectacular room at The Mount. Dennis had felt it was the ideal venue for a speech of his magnitude, but Brenda and Stinky had chosen a much smaller room, as soon as they heard the price.

"Nearly there," Dennis told him. He was busy making more notes. "I nearly forgot to mention my years has a Scout Patrol leader."

Billy reluctantly wandered back to the hotel entrance to try and sort the mess out. Dennis finished what he was doing, rolled the manuscript up as tightly as he could and wedged it into his back pocket. He heard raised voices coming from Billy's direction. One of the voices seemed strangely familiar, but Dennis took little notice, too busy thinking about his speech. Suddenly, he paused, it was as if he'd forgotten something important. He thought back to what Billy had told him, "There's another wedding, Lord and Lady somebody." At that same moment, he recognised the loud voice. He was instantly transported back many years to the Barn Dance and his traumatic meeting with Lady Gertrude. Dennis nearly fainted, then he spun around, frantically searching the now quite large crowd near the hotel entrance. He was just thinking that maybe he'd been mistaken, when he suddenly heard a loud, high pitched shrieking. Even though she was quite a distance away, the voice was unmistakable.

"Just a minute, it can't be, no, surely not, yes, yes, it is. I think it's my little ginger-haired chum, young Dennis Basket, dressed up has a soldier," she started striding towards him, shouting, "Cooweee!! Dennis Basket is that you?"

Dennis immediately used the old trick of looking around in all directions, as if he'd heard someone call but couldn't quite make out which direction it had come from. He placed his peaked cap on top of his head. He looked everywhere except in the right direction and then slowly walked around the corner of the hotel, glancing about himself, as if searching for the owner of the voice. The second he was out of sight, he sprinted as quickly as he could. Halfway along the side of the building, he spotted an open door, so he ran to it and stepped inside the building, immediately realising that he was inside a large kitchen. He could see a man in a chef's hat, working in an adjoining room, but apart from that, there was no one around. He frantically searched about him for somewhere to hide, then suddenly, he heard footsteps approaching outside and then a loud voice close by. "Did anyone spot my chum, he's a little ginger chap." She seemed to be right outside the kitchen door. Dennis spun around and there was a big, white door with a metal lever on it, right in front of him. He pushed down the lever, opened the door and stepped into the darkness, slamming the heavy door behind himself. All outside sounds disappeared, but still, for a long time, Dennis was scared to even breathe. Eventually, he could hold his breath no longer and gasped for air. *She must have gone by now*, he thought to himself and turned around to open the door. It was so dark he couldn't see a thing. He felt around, but there did not appear to be a handle on this side of the door; he also suddenly realised just how cold it was. The sweat on his brow was now freezing cold. He started to feel a bit concerned and waved his hands around in the darkness. Instantly, his hand touched what initially appeared to be a spider's web. He jumped backwards, but has he did so, he realised it was in fact a piece of string hanging down from above him. He felt around again, and on locating it, he pulled downwards, and a dull light came on. Dennis looked about him, he was in a small room, there were cardboard boxes stacked up in one corner, a large piece of beef hanging from a hook and on shelves, a variety of metal trays covered in some sort of cloth. He walked over and looked underneath, some held meats and others pork pies and sausage rolls. "I'm stuck inside a big fridge," he muttered to himself and then started hopping around to keep warm.

Billy looked around, but Dennis was nowhere to be seen. *Typical*, he thought to himself, *he's gone off to prepare for his big speech and left me to do all the work.*

He checked inside the big room where the reception was being held. Although there was no sign of Dennis, he was delighted to see a large buffet table being loaded with trays of food by two ladies wearing long white aprons. He looked around, and whilst their backs were turned, he quickly grabbed a pork pie and rammed it into his mouth. His screams could be heard all around the hotel as hot fat squirted out and ran down his chin. He spat the pie out as quickly as he could. In the centre of the nearest table was a vase of flowers. Billy ripped the flowers out of the vase, gulped down some of the water and poured the rest over his head. He turned to see the two women staring at him.

"Bit warm in here," he gasped, "maybe we should open a window."

The lady nearest to him said,

"Be careful with those pies; they're just out the oven."

Billy nodded and then walked back outside, fanning his mouth with his hand. Just as he reached the hotel entrance, a car pulled up, and a smiling Stinky stepped out. A small crowd of guests cheered and started to throw confetti. Stinky suddenly realise he was on his own. He glanced back and saw Brenda giving him a disapproving look through the car window. He ran back and opened a car door, shouting, "Sorry, my love." Brenda stepped out and took his arm. The guests commenced cheering again as the happy couple walked passed them, and into the hotel. Billy ran after them and explained that the Best Man was missing but should turn up at any moment.

Dennis was starting to get worried now. He clapped his hands together and jumped up and down. Clouds of white breath came from his mouth. He pulled his peaked army cap down as far as he could until suddenly, the peak came away in his hand.

"Great," he muttered to himself. "Buckethead is going to love that, a peaked cap, with no peak."

On a shelf, he noticed a large, folded white cloth. He grabbed it and wrapped it around his shoulders, like a big shawl.

This is a disaster, he thought. O*bviously, they will have to delay the reception, if I'm not there to do the vital Best Man's speech.*

"Well, it looks like you will have to do the Best Man's speech," Brenda said to Billy.

Billy looked shocked.

"Me, why me? Dennis should be here any moment."

Stinky nodded in agreement.

"Give it another few minutes, my love," he said to his new wife. "Dennis will be devastated; he's been preparing this speech since he was about five." But as he looked around the room, he could see guests were starting to get restless; some were glancing at the watches, he knew he could wait no longer. He placed a reassuring arm on Billy's shoulder and said.

"I know you haven't prepared a speech Billy, but Brenda and I really need you to save the day," He saw the look on Billy's face, so he said the one thing that he knew would inspire him.

"The sooner we get this speech done, the sooner we can get stuck into all this food."

Billy immediately sprang into action.

He leapt up and banged the table with his glass of beer and then mumbled an apology as much of it splashed over Brenda's wedding dress.

"Ladies and Gentlemen," he whispered and then cleared his throat, as someone shouted, "Speak up, we can't hear you."

Billy tried to think of something to say as the tables full of guests stared back at him.

"It's very nice of you all to be here today for the wedding of Brenda and Stinky, oops, I mean Jack," he began and then noticed the large table groaning with food and added.

"Of course, if you hadn't turned up, there would have been a lot more food for me."

Everybody laughed, and Stinky clapped him on the back.

This isn't too bad after all, he thought to himself and continued.

"First of all, I'd like to thank Brenda for asking Jack to marry her, and Jack for agreeing to do it."

For some reason, this got everyone laughing again and raising their glasses.

Billy couldn't believe it. For once he was the centre of attraction. He managed to recall a few old stories, mainly from their Scouting days, but soon ran out of things to say, so, he concluded with.

"Lastly, I'd just like to give a special mention to Dennis Bisskit, who has worked very hard on a much bigger speech, but, unfortunately, appears to have disappeared." Someone in the crowd, who obviously knew Dennis, shouted, "That's a lucky break."

Billy then asked the crowd to raise their glasses and join him in a toast to the happy couple. Which they happily did, and then they cheered and clapped as Billy sat down.

Dennis banged on the fridge door and shouted, but no one seemed to be listening. High on the far wall, a large fan would start whizzing around every few minutes, and a new blast of freezing air would enter the room. Icicles were starting to form around the rim of his hat. He felt terrible knowing that Stinky, Brenda and all the guests must be just standing around, waiting for him to make his big entrance. He was fairly certain that without his magnificent speech the whole reception would probably have to be called off. To keep himself occupied, he went over the first few pages of his manuscript.

"Ladies and Gentlemen, I am Dennis Winston Bisskit, the Best Man. Just to tell you a little bit about myself, I was born in 1945, in Dudley, on the day the war ended. My parents are George and Edith Bisskit. My father was wounded in a top-secret

146

mission; my grandfather is also a war hero. He got this medal in France…"

Even though he was standing on his own in a large fridge, he pointed at the borrowed medal which was hanging from his jacket and imagined the rapturous applause. It was always best to rehearse properly.

His teeth were now chattering so badly, that he couldn't carry on speaking. It suddenly occurred to him that this could be the end.

"I can't let it happen," he chattered, "the nation needs me too much, and how could Sticky possibly cope without me?"

He recommenced banging on the door.

Meanwhile, not far away, Billy was starting to feel a bit sick. Fearing that somehow the food would run out, he'd crammed as much into his mouth as he could. Anything and everything: several large slices of cheese and potato Flan, sausages on little sticks, his favourite Pork Pies and lots of assorted sandwiches. He even tried a salmon sandwich. He'd never tried salmon before, and after he'd finished it, he decided that he never wanted to try it again. Soon it would be time to move on to desserts, and of course, wedding cake and although that was an exciting prospect, Billy had decided that he needed one last Pork Pie. Unfortunately, just as he reached the table, someone grabbed the last one off the plate. Billy just stood there, feeling a bit despondent, but then a waitress came over and started removing some of the empty plates.

"Excuse me, sorry to bother you," he said. "I'm Billy, the Best Man. I was just wondering if there were any more Pork Pies."

She looked annoyed at first, but at least he'd asked politely, unlike some people, so she replied.

"There may be a tray in the cool room; I could soon warm them up. I'll just pop and check."

Billy watched her walk across the room and then looked around. Everyone seemed in good spirits, laughing and enjoying themselves. He was just wondering what had become of Dennis when his thoughts were shattered by a piercing scream, then a woman's voice shouted.

"Help, come quick, somebody help me."

Upon opening the cool room door, the waitress had been met by a truly horrifying sight. A young man in army uniform stood before her. He was wearing the remains of a military hat; the peak appeared to have disappeared. He had pulled it down so far that it covered his eyes. He also had a large white shawl draped around his shoulders. He was covered in patches of frost and had several icicles hanging from his nose. His right hand grasped tightly onto a roll of papers, and he kept muttering something, but his teeth chattered so badly that it was impossible to make out just what he was trying to say. On hearing her cries for help, guests had run to see what was wrong. A couple of them grabbed Dennis and carried him out of the cool room. They tried to sit him down in a chair, but he appeared to be frozen upright so, instead, they just laid him down on the floor. Stinky ran into the room and couldn't believe his eyes.

"What were you doing, playing in there? You've missed the food."

The waitress said a doctor was staying at the hotel, so she rushed off to find him, whilst someone placed a thick blanket over the frozen Dennis. Brenda had joined her new husband, and they crouched down to reassure their friend that he was in safe hands now. Dennis moved his head up to look in their direction. He moved very slowly as if his neck needed oiling. Then he quietly stammered.

"Sp..sp.sp.."

"Shush everyone, he's trying to speak," Brenda shouted.

"Sp..sp..sp.." Dennis tried again.

Stinky got down on his knees and leaned closer.

"What is it Ginge, what are you trying to say?"

Dennis slowly moved his eyes down, gave a slight nod at the roll of papers in his hand and tried again.

"Sp..sp..sp.."

Stinky had to prise Dennis's frozen fingers back until he could release what they held. He opened the roll of papers and has he read the first page, a smile came to his face.

"Dennis, you silly sausage," he stood and turned to the crowd of guests. "It's just his speech; he's been worried about."

He turned back and looked down at his friend.

148

"You don't need to worry about that. Billy has already made the speech and it went very well. Some people are saying it was the finest speech they have heard."

Some of the crowd nodded and shouted.

"Yes, it was an excellent speech."

A tear slowly rolled down Dennis's face, before freezing to his cheek.

Brenda dabbed it with her handkerchief and said.

"Oh, isn't he sweet. He's so pleased for Billy that it's brought tears to his eyes."

Stinky threw the epic speech into a wastepaper bin.

"You don't have to worry about that any more, Ginge. You just rest up, whilst we finish the food."

***

Dennis was so engrossed in his traumatic memories that he was surprised to suddenly remember that he was in Stinky and Brenda's house. Gloria was holding his hand.

"That's a very sad story, Dennis," she said, although he could see she was trying not to laugh.

He glanced across at the sofa opposite. Stinky and Brenda were rolling about with tears running down their cheeks. Stinky suddenly stopped laughing and stood up.

"Don't worry, Ginge, the next time I get married, you will definitely make the speech," Then he quickly left the room before Brenda realised what he'd said. She must have forgotten because when he returned, she changed the subject and said.

"I've told Jack he has to get a proper job, one that actually makes money. This Private Investigator nonsense is sending us broke."

Dennis had asked Gloria to try and change the subject if this happened, so she immediately shouted,

"Oh, I meant to ask you, Brenda, did you see they are opening a new dress shop in the High Street? There's an article about it in today's local paper." Dennis and Stinky nodded and smiled as if this was the most exciting news they had heard in a while.

"Show Brenda the article, Gloria," Dennis said, "the papers in my briefcase."

Gloria got up and fetched Dennis's briefcase from where he'd left it in the hallway. She opened it, looked inside and pulled out a mouldy cheese sandwich. Brenda just shook her head and said,

"I told you. Hopeless."

"Oh, here it is," Gloria said, removing a newspaper. As she did, something else fell to the ground next to Dennis. He picked up the photograph that Dawkins had given him a few days back, the one showing Winston, at the Xmas party.

"You may as well throw that in the bin," he said, passing it to Gloria. "We have already cleared young Winston."

Gloria stared at it, and then said,

"I know that lady, she's been to the hotel a couple of times to see Mr Taggert," She thought for a moment and then added. "Mrs Royce, that's her name."

Dennis took the photograph back from her and looked at it again. It showed Winston smiling a smile like a watermelon sitting at a table and beyond him, two other men and a miserable looking woman. He remembered Jean, the cleaning lady's description of her. "She's always got a mardy look on her face."

"I'm afraid you have her mixed up with someone else," he told Gloria. "This lady is Mrs Templer; she's in charge of cataloguing at the Gallery."

Gloria leaned closer and had another look.

"Well, I don't care what name she gave you, she definitely told me her name was Mrs Royce. I showed her to Mr Taggert's room the other day. I remember because I was walking past his room just as she left and he called her a funny name, like a nickname." She stared into space for a second and then said, "Charlie, that was it, I remember thinking it was a funny name for a woman. He shouted, 'Won't be long now, Charlie.'"

Dennis frantically searched through his briefcase until he found his notebook. He wiped some jam off the cover and flicked through the pages until he found what he was looking for.

"Charlotte, she said her name was Charlotte Templer."

The room was quiet for a moment. Brenda left for the kitchen to get apple pie and custard for dessert.

"And this Mr Taggert, what does he do?" Dennis asked.

Gloria shook her head.

"I told you all about him, he's been living at the hotel for a few weeks, he's studying the old tunnels that run under the city centre. He's writing a book about them, and it's going to be good advertising for the hotel, so they are letting him stay for free."

Dennis stared into space.

"I told you all about him last week," Gloria said.

"See, I told you, they just don't listen," Brenda shouted, as she entered the room carrying a tray.

Dennis ignored her and looked over at Stinky

"So, Mrs Templer, the cataloguer at the Art Gallery is using a false name and visiting a man who has access to tunnels running under the city centre. Are you thinking what I'm thinking Stinky?"

"I'm not sure," his friend answered. "I was thinking, I hope there's enough apple pie for seconds, is that what you were thinking?"

Dennis shook his head.

"No, that's not what I'm thinking. I'm thinking that I've had something at the back of my mind all this time and now I know what it was; it's the basement, it's always been the basement."

As usual, Stinky looked confused.

"Remember," Dennis said, "Someone had left the basement door unlocked."

Stinky shook his head.

"But we checked, nothing was stolen."

Dennis smiled. "Of course, nothing was stolen. Don't you see Stinky, we have been looking at this the wrong way. We thought the door was open because someone had gone into the basement."

Everyone was staring at him.

"The door was open because someone had come out of the basement."

Brenda placed plates of apple pie in front of them. Gloria patted Dennis on the back and whispered, "Well done," and Stinky suddenly worked it out in his head.

"They tunnelled their way into the basement," he gasped, and then added, "But you had a look around, you would have seen a hole."

"Not necessarily, remember Jane Fonda told us that something looked different down there. Did you ask her about that last night?"

Stinky tried to think. Brenda suddenly put down her spoon and said.

"Just a minute. You were with Jane Fonda last night? I thought you told me you were working."

Stinky held up his hand.

"Hang on; I'd had a few drinks by the time I asked her."

Brenda rose from her chair.

"You were out drinking with Jane Fonda last night."

Stinky suddenly remembered.

"She said that some old carpet had been moved closer to a wall."

Dennis smiled and then frowned until Gloria asked him what was wrong.

"I need Dawkins to let me have another look at that basement, and I'm completely out of M.J.K. Smith memorabilia."

He ate some apple pie.

"Wonderful pie Brenda," he said, and then noticed the look on her face.

"Cheer up Brenda; I'm sure Stinky has a perfect excuse for why he was out partying with Jane Fonda last night."

She stared at the two men and then said.

"He certainly better have, or else he'll be sleeping in the garden shed tonight. And another thing. I've told you before, will you kindly refer to my husband as Jack, you know I don't like that other name."

Dennis grinned and raised his glass to his friends.

"Absolutely. Jack, it is then, Stinky."

He stood up, and a dumpling that he'd hidden in his pocket fell out and crashed to the floor. There was a clanging sound, and then it rolled under the table. Luckily, Brenda was busy asking Stinky all about Jane Fonda.

Chapter 29

Dennis impatiently tapped his fingers on the steering wheel as Brenda gave Stinky one last hug. He gave the car horn another loud blast, and Stinky trotted down the garden path, opened the passenger side door and climbed in. As usual, he had a big smile on his face.

"Morning, Ginge."

Dennis dramatically stared at his watch and said,

"Oh, is it? I was sitting there for so long I thought it might be the afternoon by now. If you got around to buying your own car, I wouldn't have to ferry you around everywhere."

The smile never left Stinky's face.

"I was just reading in the newspaper about the big music festival on the Isle of Wight in August; they say there could be hundreds of thousands there. We should go, Ginge. A couple of wild young lads like us, we should definitely go."

Dennis looked at his reflection in the mirror, he licked the back of his hand and flattened some stray hairs down. He didn't feel like a wild young lad.

"Are The Beatles going to be there?" he asked.

"I'm afraid not," Stinky told him.

"Everyone else is though, Bob Dylan, The Who."

"Rubbish," Dennis said.

"If, The Beatles aren't playing it's not worth going. As you well know, I am probably the foremost expert on music in the Dudley area, and I'm fairly confident in saying that six months from now, no one will even remember Bob Dylan and The Who."

Stinky laughed.

"Well, this is very good news for them. Given your record, this probably means that people will still be listening to Bob Dylan and The Who fifty years from now."

"Well, hopefully, we will live long enough to see," Dennis said, "and don't think I won't track you down to some old person's home, and say I told you so."

Stinky suddenly realised they were not heading towards their office.

"I'm hoping Dawkins will let me have another look around that basement," Dennis explained.

Stinky nodded but then said.

"Are we now saying that he isn't involved at all?"

"I can't see how," Dennis replied. "If he knew about a tunnel in the basement, he wouldn't have let me look the first time. All he had to say was, he couldn't get the key. And whilst we are there, you can have another word with Jane Fonda and see what she has to say about Mrs Templer or Mrs Royce, or whatever her name is."

Stinky groaned, "Do I have to? I think that she thinks it's all just an excuse for me to get to see her, she thinks I fancy her, Ginge. Anyway, I asked her about all the staff the other night in the Red Lion." He removed his notebook from his jacket pocket and flicked through the pages before pausing.

"Yes, here we go, Mrs Templer. Evidently, she has a face like a smacked arse. Far too timid to get involved in anything legal, she wouldn't say boo to a goose."

Dennis considered this information for a while and then said.

"Well, why would she say boo to a goose? Who says boo to a goose? Have you ever said boo to a goose?"

Stinky shook his head.

"It's just an expression, Ginge."

"Well, I've never said boo to a goose, and I can't imagine any situation in the future when I would say boo to a goose. For one thing, it's totally unfair to the goose. Imagine the poor goose, just walking along minding its own business, when someone suddenly leaps out from behind a hedge and says boo!!"

He looked over at his friend to see if he agreed, but Stinky was just leaning forward holding his head in his hands, so he continued.

"No, you won't get any of that sort of behaviour from me, Stinky. In fact, when I finally pass away, it will probably be written on my gravestone."

"HERE LIES DENNIS BISSKIT

HE NEVER INDULGED IN GOOSE BOOING."

He again turned to look at Stinky, who finally looked up and said.

"Good, that's excellent news. I'm glad we have finally sorted that out Ginge. It's something that I have been really losing sleep over."

Dennis nodded.

"I'm glad you agree, Stinky."

"You mean Jack. Don't forget you promised Brenda that you would now call me Jack."

Dennis shrugged.

"If that's what you would prefer, Stinky, Jack it is, after all, like you say I did promise, Brenda." Then, as he turned away, he mumbled.

"I bet she has said boo to a few geese."

A few minutes later, they were parking outside The Art Gallery and Museum. Dennis noticed the look of fear on Stinky's face.

"Okay, we will forget about Jane Fonda for now, you can help me search the basement. Grab the torch."

They had a quick look around and soon spotted the Security Guard giving directions to an elderly lady. He didn't seem surprised to see them.

"Oh, it's you again, I spent last evening repairing the roof of my lock-up, what have you got to say for yourself?"

Dennis chuckled and shook his head.

"Please don't concern yourself with that. I know some people would involve lawyers, it is dangerous having a dodgy roof like that, but luckily no one was injured, so I'm willing to let it go. However, we would like to have another quick look in the old basement, if that's okay."

Dawkins couldn't believe his ears.

"No, it isn't okay. I shouldn't have shown you the first time. Anyway, I'm far too busy."

Dennis shrugged his shoulders.

"Fair enough. I realise you are a busy man, sorry to disturb you, come along, Stinky, let's leave Sergeant Dawkins to his work," then as he turned away, Dennis mumbled, "It is a pity though because I had something special to show you."

They had walked about five yards before Dawkins cracked.

"What do you mean, something special? Is it something of M.J.K. Smith's?"

The lads strode back. Dennis reached into his jacket pocket, but then instantly pulled his hand out again empty.

"No, I shouldn't. Uncle Jimmy gave me these on my twenty-first birthday; they mean a lot to me."

Dawkins looked like he was about to get down on his knees and beg, so Dennis pulled the item from his pocket. Dawkins gasped.

"I don't believe it, are those M.J.K. Smith's spectacles?

"The very same," Dennis said, "in fact, he wore these when he made his 121 against South Africa."

The guard stared at them lovingly and then asked if it was possible to hold them. Dennis reluctantly passed them to him.

"Please be very careful; they are priceless."

Dawkins studied them from every angle until Dennis said.

"I just keep them in a drawer at home, I suppose really they should go to someone who would look after them as they deserve to be looked after," and then as if he'd suddenly thought of it.

"I don't suppose you would be interested, Sergeant Dawkins and of course in return, we would like to have a quick look in the basement. You could just lend me the key for ten minutes. No need for you to show me the way, what with you being so busy."

It took Dawkins all of two seconds to decide. He reached into his pocket, took out a large key ring with several keys hanging from it, removed one and handed it over.

"You've got ten minutes and then return the key to me in my office and don't go touching anything."

He walked off in one direction and the lads in another. Shortly after they had left, Mrs Templer emerged from behind the large statue they had been standing next to. She felt faint. Everything was closing in. She knew she had to get away.

As they walked down corridors and steps towards the old basement, Stinky said.

"It's an amazing coincidence. I couldn't help but notice that M.J.K. Smith's spectacles bear a remarkable resemblance to your granddad's spectacles."

Dennis looked shocked and then said.

"Do you really think so? Well, I suppose one pair looks much like another pair."

They walked past the basement. Dennis explained that this was the new basement, not the old basement.

"I don't understand that," Stinky told him. "If the old basement is the lowest floor, why not just call that the basement and the new basement the ^first^ floor. I don't see how you can have two basements, one a floor higher than the other."

Dennis stopped walking to think about this and finally said.

"You're quite right, Stinky, it is strange, I don't know why I didn't think of that." It occurred to him, not for the first time that even though he was obviously the brains of the partnership, Stinky could be quite perceptive at times.

They walked down the old worn steps. Dennis turned the key in the large wooden door, and it creaked open.

Dennis reached up and pulled the cord just inside the doorway, and the dull light came on.

"Wow, it's huge," Stinky said, "We should have bought a football, we could have had a kick around."

"No time for that," Dennis told him, "Pass me the torch."

Stinky pulled his old army torch from his jacket and handed it to his friend.

"Lucky I accidentally on purpose forgot to hand this torch in when we left the army, it's come in useful."

"I'm sure they have plenty more to go around," Dennis mumbled, as he shone the torch around the room.

"This could take forever," Stinky moaned, where do we begin?"

Dennis shone the torch against a far wall and smiled.

"Oh, that's easy, my friend. Remember what Jane Fonda told you? Something was different in the basement after the robbery."

Stinky thought for a second and then saw where Dennis was shining the torch.

"Of course, the old rolls of carpet had been moved." They both ran across the room and started pulling the heavy carpets away from the wall. Then Dennis shone the torch down at the floor.

"I don't believe it," he said disappointedly, "I was certain there would be a hole to the tunnel."

Dennis stared at the ground; it was covered in what looked like decades of dirt. He looked around the room and then spotted a sturdy looking, sweeping brush with thick bristles standing amongst the cleaning supplies. He grabbed it and swept away some of the accumulated dirt, but all he found underneath was a grimy old concrete floor. He turned the brush upside down and banged the floor with the handle, but the ground was solid.

Dennis looked so disappointed that Stinky took the brush off him and moved along a few feet before striking the floor again, but once more, he just heard the sound a solid floor makes when someone hits it with a brush handle.

"It's no use," Dennis said. "I got it wrong, maybe I've been wrong about everything."

He turned away and stood sadly with his hands on his hips. Stinky went to throw the brush away, but then at the last second, moved along another couple of yards and banged the ground again.

He was so amazed that he dropped the brush. Dennis turned and shouted.

"What was that?"

Stinky picked the brush back up and struck the floor again in the same spot. The sound was completely different. There was an unmistakable echo.

"Stinky, and I rarely say this, you are a genius."

Stinky shrugged as if it were an everyday occurrence.

Dennis took the brush off him, turned it over and started sweeping the dirt away.

"Look it's a different colour, this is new cement."

He struck the surface several times, and cracks appeared as the cement shattered. Dennis swept the pieces away and then dropped the brush, got down on to his knees and started brushing the bits away with his hand.

"Look," he gasped, "there's wood underneath, it's a trapdoor."

They spent several minutes, clearing all the new cement away until they could see properly. It was obvious someone had tunnelled up from below and then gone to great trouble to hide their work.

"Look, this trapdoor fits perfectly. We would need to smash it with an axe to get through," Dennis said with admiration in his voice.

"Why go to so much trouble?" Stinky asked. "They could have just pulled the carpet over the hole. It would probably be years before anyone even noticed."

Dennis was thoughtful for a moment.

"I'll tell you why Stinky. It's because whoever did this job is a professional; he doesn't like to leave anything to chance, he doesn't make mistakes."

"But he's made one this time."

"Yes, he has," Dennis shouted, "he made the mistake of entering Planet, Bisskit and Blackshaw."

They swept the bits of broken cement back over the trapdoor and then pulled the carpets back to cover it.

"So, what happens now?" Stinky asked. "Do we call the police?"

Dennis shook his head.

"No way, we need more proof if we are to get that reward money. If we call the police now, Inspector Pratt will turn up and say, 'Thank you, lads, now get lost,' and that's the last we will hear about it, he will take all the credit. Anyway Stinky, it's not just that; it's personal. I asked Gloria to describe her Mr Taggert, and he's the same man who tried to kill me. It's not right; it's very unkind to attempt to kill someone you've never even met before."

Stinky nodded.

"Yes, you're right. Now, if he had met you, I could well understand why he'd wish to kill you."

He laughed, but then noticed the serious look on his friend's face, so he patted his shoulder and said.

"Okay, Ginge, he's not going to do that to my best friend. Let's show him you don't mess with Blackshaw and Bisskit, Private Investigators."

Dennis thanked his friend. In times of trouble, there was no one better to have by your side than Stinky.

"Come on," he said, and walked towards the doorway which led out of the basement, but halfway there he stopped and added.

"I saw what you did there, by the way. Blackshaw and Bisskit, Private Investigators, you obviously got a bit mixed up due to the excitement."

Stinky smiled and said, "Obviously."

As they walked up the steps and past the new basement, Stinky suddenly stopped and said.

"You're wrong, Ginge, you said this man doesn't make mistakes, well, he made one big one when he forgot to lock the basement door. Just think, if he'd done that we would have had no reason even to look down there and the trapdoor was so well hidden, I doubt that anyone would ever have found it."

Dennis stared for a moment and then shook his head.

"It wasn't him that made a mistake, Stinky. Think about it, if our theory is correct, the thief, probably the mysterious Mr Taggert, entered the basement through the trapdoor. Someone, probably our Mrs Templer, had left the door open for him and turned off the alarm. All he had to do was pop upstairs, taking care to avoid the night watchman, remove the painting, smash a window to look like he'd left that way, race back down to the basement and he's free. All Mrs Templer had to do was come in early, get down to the basement, put a new bit of cement down, I noticed an open bag on a shelf, then, sweep dirt back over the trapdoor, cover it with the carpets, lock the basement door, run back to the exhibition room and raise the alarm. It's brilliant, Stinky. The only trouble was, Mr Taggert may be a professional, but unfortunately for him, Mrs Templer isn't. She was in such a rush that she forgot to lock the basement door. I bet she never told Mr Taggert; he doesn't strike me has the type to tolerate mistakes."

They turned and carried on walking.

"Let's get this key back to Dawkins," Dennis said, "and then I think it's time we said hello to Mrs Templer. I want to ask her some questions and see how she reacts."

Unfortunately, when they asked Dawkins about her whereabouts, he told them that she had gone home sick about ten minutes ago.

"Seems a bit of a coincidence," Stinky said. "We come in to search the basement, and she suddenly gets sick."

The security guard shook his head.

"Surely you don't think Mrs Templer is involved. I don't believe it, she, she...," he struggled to find the words so Stinky helped him.

"We know. She wouldn't say boo to a goose."

Dawkins nodded in agreement.

"Let me ask you something, Sergeant," Dennis said. "You told me that you had the only key to the old basement and it was in its normal spot on the morning of the robbery."

Dawkins looked offended.

"Of course it was, do you think I had something to do with the theft?"

Dennis shook his head.

"Certainly not, you are ex-Staffordshire Regiment," Dennis assured him. "But is there any way Mrs Templer could have got hold of the key and maybe made a copy?"

Dawkins thought for a moment, and then a strange look came into his eyes.

"That explains it," he said. "She never normally speaks to me, probably because I'm working class, but a few weeks back she suddenly came into the office and started chatting like we were old friends. Then she came back in the afternoon and bought me a cup of tea. I couldn't believe it. After that she went back to normal, just ignoring me."

"She must have taken the key whilst you were not looking, had a copy made and returned your key later that day."

Dawkins looked stunned.

"One other thing," Dennis asked. "That morning, was she in early?"

"Of course she was," the guard replied. "She's practically lived here the last few months. The first person in, and still working away when I went home."

Dennis thanked him and said.

"Can you tell me her home address and please just keep this to yourself for the moment, Sergeant, we don't want to alert her too early."

He promised he would and also told him that if they needed any assistance, they could rely on him.

The lads raced for the car, but then Dennis said.

"I'm afraid you are going to have to get the bus to Mrs Templer's house, Stinky and keep an eye on her."

Stinky groaned.

"I really need to get a car, where are you going?"

"I'm going to The Midland Hotel, and if Mr Taggert is not around, I'm hoping Gloria will let me have a look around his room."

Stinky looked concerned.

"Is that wise, Ginge, he knows your face; he's already tried to kill you once. Maybe I should check his room."

Dennis smiled.

"Don't you worry about that, Stinky, I will be in such a good disguise that my own mother wouldn't recognise me."

Stinky looked concerned again.

"Not the pirate's outfit."

"Even better than that," Dennis reassured him.

Part 4

Chapter 30

The Scottish Man lay back on his bed and stared contentedly at the ceiling. *Nearly there*, he thought to himself.

He ran through the list in his mind. He never wrote things down; why run the risk of leaving clues behind?

He lifted his arm and checked what the time was. Soon he would meet the Frenchman and find out how much he was offering. One thing was for certain; he wouldn't be letting the painting go cheaply. This had been the big job, the one that would set him up for life.

***

Stinky ran around the corner just in time to see the Smethwick bus disappearing down the road. He checked the timetable; the next bus wasn't for half an hour. For a moment, he considered walking, but it was over three miles to the address he'd been given, and it looked like rain. He looked around and spotted a café over the road.

***

Charlotte Templer stared at her reflection in the mirror and yet again wondered how she could have been so stupid. It didn't seem fair; she had always been a good person, always done the right thing and then she had just made one mistake. No one is perfect, everyone does wrong things occasionally, but most people get away with it. She had just done one wrong thing, and it had come back to haunt her.

Four years ago, she had lived and worked in Glasgow. She had a respected job as an art curator at a private gallery. She had given up on men many years ago and lived quite happily with her mother in a pleasant two- bedroomed flat in a good area of the city.

Then it had all started to go wrong. Her beloved mother was diagnosed with an incurable disease. She had taken time off work to care for her at first, but eventually, it was obvious that her mother would have to go into a care home. She had visited a few but had not been keen on any until one day; she had come across one which was perfect in every way except for the cost. It was way more than she could really afford. She went back to full-time work, but soon her savings were gone. The manager at the care home had told her that if she couldn't pay the fees soon, there was nothing they could do. She was at her wits' end, and then the Scottish Man had turned up.

He turned up at exactly the right time. No other time in her life would she even have considered his proposal, in fact, she would instantly have called the police. Later, she would wonder about this. How he had known it was the right time. He always seemed to know everything; you could never hide anything from him.

***

Stinky sipped his tea and checked his watch. "Another ten minutes," he mumbled to himself.

Dennis sat in his car and impatiently tapped his fingers against the steering wheel. "It doesn't matter where I drive, there are always roadworks going on," he moaned, to no one in particular.

***

The Scottish Man had to admit it; he had been lucky. He was a man who didn't really believe in luck, and he certainly didn't rely on it, but despite all his organisation and professionalism, it had all started with a piece of luck.

He had been walking past the public-house one cold Glasgow evening when, on a whim, he'd decided to pop in and have a pint next to a warm fire, maybe a pork pie. He'd sat minding his own business, reading a racing paper someone had left at the table. He couldn't help but overhear the conversation between the two men at the next table. At first, he'd taken no notice and then all of a sudden; he'd realised that this could be important. He had always been like that; he saw things that other people didn't see. The two men had spoken about various jobs they'd had over the years, when the older one had suddenly started talking about working in Birmingham, building tunnels under the city centre, for a Royal Mail train. "You wouldn't believe it," he'd told his friend, "It's like another city under there, there are tunnels everywhere, some still in use, some not used anymore and some, I doubt were ever used. They go under the Town Hall, under the Art Gallery, everywhere. I'll tell you what," he laughed, "if you wanted to rob a bank, there's probably a tunnel that travels right beneath one."

The Scottish Man knew men who were interested in banks, but he wasn't one of them. No, it was the mention of The Art Gallery that had attracted his attention.

He had always been interested in art. He would have loved to be able to paint himself, but even he had to admit that his talent lay in other areas.

***

Stinky put down his empty cup, waved to the lady behind the counter and walked over the road to the bus shelter. Two minutes later, the bus turned up, and he climbed on board. The rain was getting heavier.

The car in front of Dennis slowly moved forward. *At last,* he thought, *signs of life* then it stopped again.

***

The Scottish Man collected paintings, sometimes for himself, but mainly for others, other collectors who were willing to pay up in cash and asked no questions. There were more than enough of these, and he always seemed to know how to find them. He had made a good living but still wasn't satisfied. What he needed was one big job, one that paid enough money for him to retire somewhere nice, and now sitting in a decaying pub, on a cool Glasgow night, he got lucky.

Once his friend had left the pub, the man who'd been talking about working down the tunnels sat on his own for a few minutes until suddenly, the man at the next table had said.

"Hello there, my name's Taggert, can I buy you a pint?"

He'd told the man that he couldn't help overhearing his conversation and was interested because he was an author and was thinking of writing a book about the Birmingham Tunnels. As long as the Scottish Man kept buying him drinks, the man was happy to talk about his work. He gave him a lot of useful information, but the Scottish Man didn't write anything down except for one thing, the name of the engineer who had been in charge of the project. "There's nothing he doesn't know about those tunnels," the man had told him. "He could find his way around in the dark." As he walked home from the pub, he knew that he would find this engineer and the engineer would help him. People always did. Occasionally he had to use force, but he preferred to find something else. People always had something they were hiding and wished to keep hidden, but somehow, he always managed to find out what it was. He chuckled as he remembered something. It had been like that with Charlotte Templer.

∗∗∗

Charlotte wiped the tears from her eyes and thought back to the moment she had made her big mistake.

She had first spotted the man she knew as Taggert one Friday morning in the gallery. He was admiring one of her favourite paintings, a portrait of a soldier by Robert Sivell. He was very charming and knowledgeable, and they spoke for about thirty minutes before he made his excuses and left. She remembered thinking at the time that she hoped it wouldn't be the last time she saw him. How she regretted ever thinking that.

The Gallery would close at midday on a Saturday, and she was in the habit of popping into the café next door for tea and scones. That morning, she had barely sat down when Mr Taggert entered. The café was very busy, and as soon as he spotted her, he asked if he could join her at her table. She was secretly pleased. They chatted about their favourite artists, and eventually, he mentioned that he had come into the possession of a watercolour by the well-known Scottish artist, Edward Walton. He told her that he had an interested buyer but needed it authenticated. She told him to drop by the gallery during the week, and she would be pleased to have a look, as she was quite a fan of Walton's work.

It was an excellent forgery, but a forgery none the less. There were several giveaways, but the most obvious was the date on the paperwork, that came with the painting. It was a watercolour of an ocean scene in southwestern Scotland, dated 1900, but she knew for a fact that Walton had lived in London between 1894 and 1905, and all his paintings from that period were done in southern England.

When she told Taggert that unfortunately, he had bought a worthless fake, he didn't seem remotely surprised. His exact words were, "Well, we know that, but there's no reason why my buyer should find out."

She had been so shocked that she'd asked him to leave the Gallery. When he calmly answered her, all the charm and friendliness had disappeared. He said he knew all about her mother, all about how much in debt she was in. "Just do this little job for me," he'd told her, "and your debts will disappear. Your mother will continue to receive the care she deserves." And then he'd smiled the scariest smile she had ever seen and added, "We wouldn't want anything unfortunate to happen to her, would we?"

Not long after, he had left the Gallery with a letter stating that to the best of her knowledge the painting was a genuine Walton.

The next morning, when she called to see her mother, the lady in charge thanked her for paying the money she owed, plus the next six months' fees. As it turned out, she only needed two of those months before her mother passed away.

There was no way she could stay in Glasgow, so one day she applied for a job she had seen advertised in a newspaper: Head Cataloguer for the Birmingham Art Gallery.

She kept to herself and enjoyed her job until one day she looked up and saw Taggert smiling back at her.

***

Dennis fell forward, smashing his head on top of the steering wheel. He jumped back rubbing his nose and wondering for a second where he was. "Must have fallen asleep," he muttered to himself and then heard the sound of car horns blasting out behind him. He looked up and saw the road was clear ahead. A car overtook him, and the passenger leaned out the window and shouted "Idiot" at him. "There's no need for rudeness," Dennis answered and then proceeded on his journey, to The Midland Hotel. Halfway there, he stopped off at a chemist shop to buy his disguise.

Stinky got off the bus and looked up and down the road, then he checked the piece of paper with the address written on it. He walked down the road looking for a sign and finally spotted it. He turned left, walked about fifty yards and then left again. Looking up the road, he spotted a taxi standing outside a house. The driver was putting a suitcase in the boot. Then a lady emerged from the house carrying a smaller bag. She was wearing a raincoat and a headscarf. She joined the driver who was now climbing into the car. Stinky started running, but by the time he reached the house, the taxi had driven off. Not for the first time that day he thought to himself, *I really must get a car*.

***

It had been easier than even the Scottish Man had thought. He had visited a pub that he'd been told the engineer frequented. He wasn't there, but when Taggert had explained to the barman that he was an old friend and anxious to find him, the barman had replied, "Join the queue. I suppose he owes you money?"

The Scottish man, who always knew the correct thing to say, said, "Yes, how did you guess?"

The barman shook his head in disgust. "He owes me fifty quid, and you're not the only one looking for him; evidently, he owes Jimmy Boswell, 500 hundred, and as you may know, you don't owe Jimmy money and get away with it." Taggert nodded as if he did indeed know.

"So, you've no idea where he might be?" he asked. The barman shook his head, so he added.

"Has he no friends?"

It turned out he did have a friend, who when asked had insisted he had no idea as to his whereabouts. Of course, he hadn't been asked by someone like the Scottish Man before, and it only took a few minutes before he admitted that he might know the whereabouts of the engineer after all. It turned out that the engineer, like other stupid men Taggert had known before, had a bit of a gambling problem. He had gotten himself into a big mess and had been overjoyed when the Scottish Man had promised to make all his problems go away. He'd still been concerned that Jimmy Boswell was looking for him, but the Scottish Man had just said, "Don't you worry about Jimmy, I will have a little word with him, and you won't hear from him again."

Then they had got to work. The engineer turned out to be a great asset. He had suggested that The Midland Hotel was a good base, with ready access to the tunnels, and Taggert had used the same lie, he had told the man in the pub in Glasgow. He had approached the hotel manager and told him he was writing a book on the history of the Birmingham Tunnels and the role that the Midland Hotel played in them. He had suggested that it would be great advertising for the hotel. The manager had been overjoyed and offered him a free room at the hotel. It was small and basic but perfect for his needs. The manager had even given him a set of keys to the basement. From there, you descended several sets of steps, past the pumping room that pumped fresh spring water from a well to the hotel, and down to another door that led you into the tunnels.

The first time he'd gone down there with the engineer, he couldn't believe how extensive the system was. First, you walked along a fairly new section of the tunnel containing a rail line. Luckily, it wasn't in use any more. The engineer frequently consulted his maps, and then they turned off into an older looking tunnel with no lights. The engineer passed him a torch and suggested that he purchased a couple of minor's helmets with headlamps. "That way, we keep our hands free." Taggert nodded, the man was proving useful.

The engineer kept stopping and checking the map; then he would check an old army compass. Suddenly, he stopped, looked up and said.

"We are underneath the Art Gallery and Museum."

He studied the plans which the man had provided him with. They were the building plans for The Art Gallery. Once again, he wondered just who this man was. He had given him a list of things he needed, and within days, he'd been provided with them. The Scottish man seemed to be able to obtain anything he wanted. He took his time studying the plan and then walked on a little further and shone the torch above his head. Suddenly he laughed and said, "I don't believe it." The sound echoed through the tunnel. The Scottish Man followed his gaze and spotted an old concrete tube protruding from the rock above his head.

"So, what is it?" he asked.

The engineer looked at the plan again and said,

"Unless I'm very much mistaken, we are standing directly beneath the original basement to the Art Gallery. You see that pipe?" he pointed. Taggert nodded.

"Looks like it was originally put in, in case the basement flooded or something. There must be a grill in the basement floor, and any excess water would run down here."

He shone his torch around the ground beneath them.

"There's no moisture down here, so I don't think they have that problem anymore."

"How far is the floor of the basement above us?" the Scottish Man asked.

The engineer stood on his tiptoes and shone the torch up the pipe.

"Not far, about three feet. It looks like they have covered the hole with a slab of concrete. We just need the proper tools, and it wouldn't take long to dig a hole large enough for a man to get through. Of course, your main problem is that you are going to need an inside man at the Art Gallery. You really need to check the basement out to be certain we have the correct spot; also, it would make a bit of noise. No one would hear anything down here, but up there I'm not sure. You could do with a man who works there to let you know what's going on."

The Scottish Man smiled.

"It's taken care of."

"What do you mean, you already have a man?" the engineer enquired.

Taggert stared back at him, and the man turned away, realising that he'd probably asked one question, too many. The

Scottish Man already had the problem sorted. There was no need for the engineer to know that instead of finding an inside man, he'd found an inside woman, and one to whom he didn't even need to explain the consequences of not helping him.

Chapter 31

The Scottish Man yawned and looked at his watch. He sat up and rose from the bed.

Time to meet The Frenchman, he thought to himself, *let's see what he has to offer me.*

As always, he looked around the room for several minutes to make sure there was nothing to be seen that shouldn't be seen. The first day he'd moved into the hotel he had explained that he didn't want the room cleaning, he would take care of it himself. He had told the manager that he would have maps and plans and his notes lying around, and he wouldn't want them touched. He was sure that the cleaning ladies were glad not to have another room to clean, but still. He had one last look; you can never be too careful.

***

Gloria walked through the hotel foyer. It was a quiet morning, just a couple sitting waiting for a taxi. Then, as she looked around, she spotted a man sitting on his own. At first, she could not help staring, and then feeling guilty she turned away, feeling terribly sorry for the gentleman. He had obviously been in some terrible accident. He was wearing a trilby and dark glasses, but it failed to hide the fact that his face was completely covered in bandages.

Unfortunately, she had to walk past him, so she faced straight ahead, wondering if maybe he had been badly burnt in a fire. Just as she neared him, she couldn't help but take a quick glance and was horrified to see him beckon her with a wave of his hand.

She took a deep breath to compose herself and walked towards him.

"Yes sir, can I be of any assistance?"

Through the small gap in the bandages where the man's mouth was, she heard.

"You certainly can Gloria, it's me, Dennis."

Gloria couldn't believe it.

"What are you doing, Dennis, I thought you were The Invisible Man?"

She couldn't see it, but Dennis smiled beneath the bandages.

"Excellent, my disguise works, that's exactly who I'm supposed to be."

"Well, it's nice to see you, but is there any special reason why you are disguised as the Invisible Man?"

Dennis looked around the foyer and then asked her if she knew where Taggert was.

"He's gone out," she told him, "I was outside helping a lady with her bags, and he drove past me, about ten minutes ago."

"I need to see his room," he told her, "I know it's asking a lot, but we really need to get some evidence that proves his involvement."

She only thought about it for a few seconds and then said.

"Give me a moment and then follow me up those stairs," she pointed as she spoke.

Dennis watched her walk over to the reception desk, check that no one was looking and then remove some keys from a drawer. She then walked to the big staircase and waited for Dennis. She was amazed to see him hobbling towards her using a walking cane for assistance. At one point, a lady rushed over and asked him if he needed any help, but he politely refused. Gloria heard him say,

"That's very nice of you, but I need to do this myself, or else I would never leave the house."

The lady shook her head in admiration and muttered.

"You're a brave man."

"That was an amazing performance," Gloria told him.

Dennis nodded his bandaged head and mumbled.

"As you well know, I have been called the Laurence Olivier of Dudley."

She opened the door to Taggert's room and handed Dennis the key.

"Don't' get caught or else I'm in big trouble. I will be in the foyer when you've finished."

He stepped inside, closed the door behind him and checked that it was locked. He didn't move; he just looked all around the room. Disappointingly, at first glance, there was little to see. It was a small room, a battered-looking wardrobe against one wall, a small table with two chairs under it, a double bed that looked like it had seen better days. Above it on the wall a large picture, showing a scene from what looked like a desert island: white sand, turquoise water, a couple lay sunbathing on a large towel, whilst a native woman with flowers in her long, black hair, was leaning over, passing them cool drinks from a tray. Dennis glanced up and looked out of the window, all he could see was grey skies and rain. He looked back at the picture and thought how good it would be, to be on that desert island with Gloria.

He shook his head, time to concentrate. Either side of the bed were a couple of small cupboards, with lamps on top. He leaned his walking stick against the wall next to one of them and opened the bottom drawer; it was empty. He did the same with the top drawer and found all it contained was a Bible. He checked the other cupboard and found that was empty. Next to the bed was a pair of shoes, standing exactly side-by-side as if Buckethead had screamed, "Get those feet together," at them. Gloria had told him that no cleaners were allowed in his room, but you'd never have known, it was spotless, the bed was made immaculately.

This man is ex-military, Dennis thought to himself and then wondered whether it was even worth looking any further, "He won't leave anything lying around," he muttered.

***

The Scottish Man strode towards his car, stood there for a moment and then banged the roof so violently that passers-by looked over, took one glance at him and looked the other way. He opened the car door and got in. He had arranged to meet The Frenchman at another nearby hotel, not wishing him to know where he was staying. A time had been set, and then when he's arrived, there was a message waiting for him, "Sorry been delayed. Will be there an hour late. Hope it's not an inconvenience."

"Yes, it is an inconvenience," he mumbled. The Scottish Man prided himself on always being punctual, and he expected the same from others. He would make The Frenchman pay extra for this. He sat there for a few seconds, took a deep breath, and drove back to the Midland Hotel.

***

Dennis opened the wardrobe. There were some clothes hanging there: a pair of trousers, couple of shirts, a jacket. He noticed they were all perfectly ironed. He checked the pockets of the shirts and the jacket but wasn't surprised when he found them empty. At the bottom of the cupboard was a basket holding some socks and underpants, and next to that a small bag. He opened it and checked its contents: shaving stuff, toothpaste and brush, nothing out of the ordinary. He looked under the threadbare rug next to the bed and then climbed on a chair and looked on top of the wardrobe; an old suitcase sat on top of it. He took it down and studied it. No labels attached, nothing written on it. He opened the lid and looked inside, nothing, not even dust. He put it back on top of the wardrobe, carefully placed the chair back where it had been and looked around the room for several minutes. Not knowing that Taggert had done precisely the same thing, a short time earlier. He wanted to make sure he left the room as he'd found it. Then, for some reason, he walked back to the cupboard on the left of the bed, opened the drawer and took out the bible. It looked like it had been there for many years. He wondered how many lonely guests had taken comfort from it. He flicked through the pages and was just about to put it down when a small piece of paper fell from it and floated to the floor.

***

Gloria was certain that her heart stopped for a second. She had just answered the telephone at the reception desk, and when she looked up, Mr Taggert was just about to climb the stairs leading up to his room. She only caught a glimpse of his face, but it was enough to tell her he was not in a good mood. She raced after him, but when she reached his corridor, he was already putting the key in his lock.

Dennis picked up the piece of paper and read the scrawled handwriting. There was a name, DONALD FAIRCLOUGH, and then next to it the initials, ENG, and then a phone number. Dennis smiled. "You don't make many mistakes, but then you only have to make one," he whispered to himself, and then he heard a voice shouting, he recognised it straight away as Gloria.

"Mr Taggert, do you need fresh sheets?"

Dennis placed the Bible back in the drawer and quietly closed it as he heard an unmistakable Scottish accent, reply.

"No lass, it's not worth it, I'll probably be leaving tomorrow," then the door opened.

***

It took Stinky ten minutes to find a telephone kiosk. Luckily, there was a card taped above the phone with the cab number printed on it. He dialled the number, and a lady with a pleasant voice said, "Good Morning, TOA Taxi's, how may I help you?"

"Oh, good morning," Stinky replied, "I wonder if you can help me, I'm in a bit of a mess."

"I'll certainly do my best," she answered

"I've come all the way up from London to visit my mother. I wanted to surprise her because it's her birthday and you wouldn't believe it, but as I came around the corner, she was just disappearing in one of your taxis. I wondered if it's possible for you to tell me where she was heading so that I can go after her."

The woman hesitated.

"That is unfortunate, but I'm afraid I'm not supposed to give out information like that over the phone."

Stinky put on his most understanding voice.

"I understand, I wouldn't want to get you into trouble. I haven't seen her for six months, I've been too busy, but she's been unwell lately, and I was hoping to cheer her up with a surprise visit. Still, thank you for your help anyway."

He held the phone for a few seconds until he heard her say.

"Oh well, just this once I don't suppose it would do any harm. Can you give me her name and address?"

Stinky read the address he had written on a piece of paper and then said, "Her name's Charlotte Templer. I'm Jack Templer by the way."

There was quiet for a few moments, whilst she must have been checking bookings and then she came back to the phone, and he heard her chuckle.

"Well, you're not going to believe this. You came up here to surprise her, and it looks like she's gone down to London to surprise you. Our driver dropped her at the Railway Station. He helped her with her suitcases, she only just made the express to London."

Stinky thanked the lady for all her help and put the phone down. He stared at it for a moment.

It looks like Charlotte has gone into hiding, he thought to himself.

***

The Scottish Man slammed his door shut, threw his keys onto the bed and then followed them. He was a thickset man, and the mattress had seen better days, so it sagged down until it was only an inch above Dennis's nose.

Dennis lay perfectly still under the bed and tried to think what he could do if Taggert discovered him. His trilby had fallen off his head as he lay down, so he carefully placed it back on his head and pulled it down tightly over his bandages which still covered his face.

After a moment of thought, he decided that should he be discovered, firstly, he would just pretend to be asleep. Hopefully, Taggert would just think he was mad, and then if he was forced to wake up, he would speak a foreign language, he didn't actually know any foreign languages, so he would have to improvise. He hoped that the man would see his bandages and assume he was a foreign visitor who had been in a terrible accident which had left him with a preference for sleeping under a bed but incapable of finding his own room. *It just might work*, he thought.

The Scottish Man looked at his watch again. He had always been an impatient man. The mattress sagged beneath him. "Can't wait to be sleeping in a decent bed," he muttered and then bounced up and down several times. He stopped, suddenly feeling hungry, looked at his watch again, and said, "Just time for a bacon sandwich." He grabbed his room keys, had a quick glance around and left his room.

Dennis heard the door lock. He rubbed his sore nose where the springs had hit it several times. It had taken all his willpower not to cry out. He didn't dare move for a while and then suddenly he heard a loud banging on the door, followed by Gloria shouting.

"Dennis are you there? He's gone."

Dennis opened the door, and Gloria gave him a big hug.

"I was so scared, how come he didn't see you?" she asked.

"Come on Gloria, think about it," Dennis said, with more bravado than he felt.

"How can you see the Invisible Man?"

***

The Scottish Man bit into his bacon sandwich and wiped some tomato ketchup from his chin. *Not bad*, he thought, and then suddenly stopped and put the sandwich down on his plate.

Something was wrong. He always knew, his mother had called it his sixth sense. He went over everything that had happened in the last hour. There was something, something at the back of his mind, but try as he might he couldn't quite reach it. He was suddenly overcome with a feeling of doom, which had never happened to him before. He stood up, knocking his chair over, and stormed out of the café. He quickly drove to his meeting with The Frenchman. He had never felt so anxious to get back to Scotland.

Dennis raced back to the office and opened the door just in time to see Stinky putting the phone down. He didn't look very happy.

"What's wrong?" Dennis asked.

"That was Mrs Turner," Stinky told him.

Dennis had to think for a moment and then remembered that Mrs Turner had hired them to keep an eye on her husband whom she suspected of having an affair. There had been so much going on lately, he'd forgotten all about her.

"I'm afraid it's bad news," Stinky told him.

"Well, don't worry about that for now. I have good news, so we should hear that first." Stinky wasn't convinced.

"I thought if there was good news and bad news, you should always hear the bad news first."

Dennis shook his head.

"No, that's where you're wrong, if you hear the bad news first, it will put you in a bad mood and you won't enjoy the good news, whereas if you hear the good news first, you are in a good mood, so the bad news doesn't bother you quite as much."

He stared at Stinky who, knowing that he'd never yet won an argument with his friend, shrugged his shoulders and said, "Fine, let's hear your good news."

Dennis proceeded to tell him all about his morning and how close he'd come to getting caught in Taggert's room. Stinky seemed more impressed with Dennis's disguise.

"The Invisible Man, that's genius Ginge."

"Well, as you know, I am the master of disguise."

Stinky suddenly had a thought.

"You know what Ginge, I've never really thought about it before, but when people can't see Invisible Man, that means he must be naked. He's only invisible when he takes his clothes off. What if he was walking down the road and his invisibleness suddenly wore off, he would be naked in the street. Everyone could see him."

Dennis looked shocked.

"You're right Stinky; I'd never thought of that before. I always wanted to be the Invisible Man as well, but I'm not going to walk naked down the street, I might see someone I know."

"Anyway, this is all very interesting," Stinky said, "and I'm glad Taggert didn't catch you but is that your big good news?"

Dennis shook his head, reached into his pocket and pulled out the piece of paper.

He passed it to his friend and said.

"Our friend Mr Taggert made his first mistake. His room was spotless, but I found this hidden in a Bible, in his room."

Stinky stared at it and then muttered.

"Donald Fairclough, who is he, and what does ENG mean?"

"Dennis took the piece of paper back off his friend and read it again. It must be an abbreviation. Maybe it's short for English."

"Or Engelbert Humperdinck," Stinky shouted. Looking pleased with himself.

Dennis stared at him.

"Why on earth would it be Engelbert Humperdinck? What person in their right mind would be hiding a reference to Engelbert Humperdinck in a bible? It just defies logic, Stinky."

Stinky shrugged his shoulders, but then had a far more sensible thought.

"ENG, it could be short for Engineer."

"That's it Stinky," Dennis said, leaping to his feet. "I take back everything I've ever said about you my friend; you are a genius. I've been wondering how Taggert would have found his way around underground, from what I've been told, if you didn't know where you were going, you could very easily get lost. He found himself an engineer, someone who knew his way around."

Stinky smiled and then said.

"We should talk to this Donald Fairclough; we need to confirm it."

Dennis nodded his head.

"Absolutely, but first things first, we have had the good news, and I now feel mentally ready to hear your bad news."

"Its Mrs Turner, she is refusing to pay us any money. She says last night her husband confessed everything to her."

Dennis pulled a face.

"Well, I'm very pleased for her, but what's that got to do with us?"

"Well, as you know," Stinky explained. "I was dragging the job out a bit to make extra money. Well, evidently, Mr Turner told her exactly which nights he'd met his secretary and taken her to a hotel. She says we couldn't have been doing our job or else we would have known this."

The lads stared at each other and then Dennis spoke.

"Of course, she is correct Stinky; we will tell her she doesn't owe us anything, and this should be a lesson to us. From now on we will always promise to be honest with our clients, in fact, I'm going to write it down."

He took a notepad and pencil from the top drawer of their desk and wrote.

BISSKIT AND BLACKSHAW PRIVATE INVESTIGATOR, RULES.

182

RULE NO 1…ALWAYS BE TOTALLY HONEST WITH CLIENTS.

He chewed on the end of his pencil for a few seconds, and then said,

"Remember what Dick Barton used to say at the end of his radio show?"

Stinky nodded enthusiastically and said,

"Of course, make that Rule No 2."

Dennis wrote.

RULE NO 2…ALWAYS BE KIND TO OLD PEOPLE AND ANIMALS.

Then Stinky blurted out.

"What about clean underpants Ginge. My mum always used to say don't leave the house without clean underpants. That should be Rule No. 3."

Dennis thought about it,

"My mum used to say the same thing, why did they say that?"

"My mum told me it was just in case I had an accident, Ginge."

"Well, I don't know about you, but I already wear clean underpants every time I leave the house and as you well know, I have probably had more accidents than anyone else in the country, and I have to say, Stinky, in all honesty that, after I have had those accidents, I have not noticed any benefit whatsoever from the fact that I had clean underpants on."

Then he noticed the look of disappointment on his friend's face, so he quickly added.

"Still, it can't do any harm," and he wrote.

RULE NO. 3: ALWAYS WEAR CLEAN UNDERPANTS WHEN LEAVING THE HOUSE.

He was pleased to see the smile on his friend's face, but then dropped the notepad on the desk and shouted.

"What are we doing? We haven't got time for this sort of thing now; we have important work to do."

Dennis sat behind the desk, checked the phone number on his piece of paper and instructed Stinky to sit down and observe the maestro at work. He dialled the number, and a moment later a voice said.

."Hello, who's there?"

Dennis put on his posh voice and said,

"Hello, is that Mr Fairclough, Mr Donald Fairclough?"

The suspicious sounding voice answered.

"Why, who wants to know?"

"Sorry to disturb you, Mr Fairclough," Dennis replied, "I represent The Ashington Mining Company, based in South Wales, you've probably heard of us."

The man mumbled that he hadn't, but Dennis ignored him.

"The company is searching for a Chief Engineer for a new venture; you were recommended by an old work colleague." Dennis shuffled some papers on his desk as if he were searching. "Sorry, I've lost the name, it's somewhere here. Anyway, following his recommendation, I know the company would be very interested in offering you this highly paid position."

Donald Fairclough couldn't believe it. Taggert had paid off all his debts, given him a cash bonus for his assistance, and then told him to lay low for a while. But he had to admit; the Scottish Man scared him. He was afraid that Taggert might suddenly start to think that he didn't want a man around who knew all about the theft of the painting. He had been wondering about disappearing somewhere for a few months, and now the perfect answer had come calling.

"Of course," Dennis said, interrupting his thoughts. "We will need your resume. Now, I understand you have a lot of underground experience."

"Many, many years," Fairclough replied, "in fact, I spent many years as Chief Engineer on the Birmingham Tunnels; now that was a big job."

Dennis tried to sound impressed.

"Wow, you must know those tunnels like the back of your hand."

"Probably better than anyone," he answered proudly.

"That sounds ideal, Mr Fairclough," Dennis told him, "you sound like the ideal man for the job," Then he told him that he would talk to his bosses and would be in touch in the next few days. He put the phone down, looked at Stinky and said.

"Well, I might not be in touch, but I have a feeling the police will be."

Stinky smiled and said, "Nice work Ginge," and then added, "How about rule four. Stinky gets to drive the car once a week."

Dennis smiled back and said. "Steady now, I gave you the clean underpants, don't push your luck."

Stinky looked thoughtful.

"There's one thing that worries me Ginge. If Taggert is our man, and it certainly looks like he is, why is he still hanging around the hotel? If it was me that had stolen the painting, I'd want to get as far away as I could, as quickly as possible."

Dennis had already considered this and thought he knew the answer.

"Well, I don't think he's got rid of the painting yet. Once that's done, then I'm sure he will disappear. But also, I think Mr Taggert, thinks a bit like I do."

Stinky stared at him, so he explained.

"Remember when we first became friends and you introduced me to the joys of knocking on someone's front door and running away, just to annoy them."

Stinky smiled.

"Those were great days Ginge, we should knock on someone's door and run off tonight, after work, just for old times' sake."

Dennis continued.

"Now, you told me to knock on the door and run off as quickly as you could, but I seem to recall that a couple of times, the man who opened the door chased us and caught us because he was a faster runner than we were. Another time you ran so quickly that you tripped over the kerb and ripped the skin off your knee."

Stinky nodded.

"I still have the scar."

"So, one day I said to you. Now let's try it my way," Dennis added. "We knocked on the door and then walked slowly along the pavement. That man shot out of the house and asked if we had knocked on his door. I said of course not if we had done it; we would have run away."

Stinky remembered it well and laughed.

"Yes, he even apologised to us and then ran off down the road trying to find whoever knocked on his door, but what's that got to do with Taggert?"

"Taggert is like me; he's knocked on the Art Gallery door, so to speak, and hung around nearby, probably so he can laugh at the police searching all over the country for him. Once it all dies down, he will be off; we need to stop him before he goes."

Stinky hesitated and then said.

"You sound like you admire him, Ginge."

"He's a very bad person, Stinky, but I can still appreciate his skill at what he does. He is Moriarty to my Sherlock Holmes."

"And don't forget, to my Doctor Watson," Stinky shouted.

"Quite so, my friend, quite so."

***

The Scottish Man sat back in his car. The meeting had gone very well. They had played the usual game. The Frenchman had at first tried to downplay his interest in the painting, even though they both knew Picasso was his favourite. Then, he had tried to say that the market for high-quality paintings was flat at the moment. Eventually, he had asked The Scottish Man just how much he was asking. The Scottish Man had named an exorbitant price; the Frenchman had laughed and offered half, then they had negotiated until eventually, they had agreed on the exact price that the Scottish Man had wanted all along.

In the morning, he would deliver the painting. The Frenchman would study it, and then he would get his money. They had done business before; they trusted each other.

He headed back towards the hotel, and then suddenly felt that a small celebration was in order. He parked up, strode into an upmarket pub and ordered an expensive whiskey. He found himself a seat against the back wall where he could keep an eye on anyone entering and took a sip of his drink. "Life is good," he muttered to himself, and then he quickly thought through any loose ends he had to take care of before the morning.

The painting was already in a safe place. He would go over his room very carefully, to make sure nothing incriminating was left behind, then he just had one last trip to make down the tunnels to retrieve a bag he'd hidden. He could just leave it down there, it might never be found, but that was not the way he worked.

He watched, as an elderly man in a raincoat shuffled through the door, he struggled to walk, even with the aid of a walking stick.

The Scottish Man had just been about to take a sip of his drink but has he raised his glass, he suddenly stopped. A walking stick, that was it. That was what had been gnawing at the back of his mind all morning. He thought back. He had returned to his room early when his meeting with The Frenchman had been delayed. He replayed it in his mind. He had decided to go and get something to eat. He had gone to open the door and quickly glanced around his room, and now, in his mind, he saw it, a walking stick leaning against the wall next to his bed. For some reason, it had not registered at the time. Maybe because he had been so annoyed at The Frenchman. He leapt up and strode out of the pub and to his car. As he drove towards the Midland Hotel, he suddenly had another memory. This morning when he had left for his meeting, a man, with his head covered in bandages had limped past his car, he'd been using a walking stick. At the time, The Scottish Man had paid little attention. He tried to picture the man. He was obviously unrecognisable, but one thing that stood out was his short stature. He parked his car and sat there for a while wondering what it all meant, and then he smashed his fist down on the steering wheel.

"The little ginger man. I underestimated him."

He raced up the hotel stairs, opened the door to his room, flung it open and stood in the doorway. He carefully looked all around. As he had expected, there was no walking stick leaning against his wall, but he didn't for one second think he was mistaken. He slowly walked to the table, pulled out one of the chairs and sat down. Nothing looked any different. He prided himself on being organised; he cleaned his room every day, he liked to be certain that if he had to make a sudden move, he'd leave nothing incriminating behind. He rubbed his chin. *So, if it was Ginger, how could he have found me?* he thought to himself. He looked at it from every angle and eventually smiled. That was it; it was just bad luck. There was no way Ginger could have linked him to the robbery and traced him to this hotel. So, it was all to do with the car. The Scottish Man was professional enough to admit he'd made a mistake. When he had entered the enemy's territory to booby-trap his car, he obviously should have worn a disguise. He had been so confident that the crash would incapacitate the young investigator that he'd even stared at him and smiled as he'd driven past. By pure chance, Ginger must have been driving past the hotel and spotted him entering. Maybe he'd quickly followed him and seen which room he went into, put on that stupid disguise, somehow got hold of a key, or more likely picked the lock and entered his room.

Now he thought about what it all meant. At first, he considered moving to another hotel overnight, until he got his money. Then the more he thought about it, the more he felt that the ginger man didn't actually know anything at all. If he'd really recognised him, surely the first thing he'd have done was call the police. They would have been waiting for him when he'd returned to the hotel. No, he could see it all now. Ginger had thought it was him but couldn't be certain. He'd searched his room and found nothing. He'd probably ask a member of staff about him, and they would say. "He's an author; he's here writing a book. He's always very polite and well behaved," and Ginger would think he'd made a mistake; he'd just seen someone who looked like the man who'd cut his brake cable.

He took a deep breath and slowly relaxed. "Nothing to worry about, but I must be more careful in the future," he muttered to himself.

The man who normally never made mistakes had made another one.

***

Dennis and Stinky sat in the park, eating their sandwiches. They had decided it was too nice a day to stay in the office. They walked to the park, found a bench and leaned back, enjoying the warmth.

Stinky opened his brown paper bag, looked inside and pulled a face.

"Spam again, I'm sick of Spam."

Dennis immediately turned to him and handed over his bag containing his cheese and chutney sandwiches, whilst his friend gave him his bag.

"I don't understand why you can't just tell Brenda that you don't like Spam," Dennis told him.

Stinky shook his head.

"I can't do it. Spam sandwiches were the first sandwiches she ever made me. I said they were wonderful, I didn't have the heart to tell her that I couldn't stand Spam, and now I can never tell her or she will know that I lied to her."

Dennis nodded, he thought he understood.

"Well, in that case, it's just lucky for you that I don't care if I eat Spam or cheese and chutney."

They finished each other's sandwiches, threw a few crumbs to the gathering flock of birds at their feet and discussed what to do next.

"I think it's time we went to the police," Stinky said.

Dennis wasn't certain.

"I just wish we had found the painting, without that Taggert might still be able to talk his way out of it."

***

The man they were discussing had felt so confident he had fallen asleep for a couple of hours. He woke with a start and looked at his watch, it told him it was 3pm. *Another few hours and I'm a very wealthy man*, he smiled at the thought. Then he thought back to what had happened earlier. He still felt confident that there was nothing to worry about, but he hadn't got where he was today by not being thorough. He had called the Art Gallery yesterday, telling the lady who answered that he was an old friend of Charlotte Templer and he wished to speak to her. He had just wanted to make sure that she understood the consequences of ever revealing what she knew about the theft of the painting. The lady had told him that Charlotte had taken some leave. She had gone home with a cold and the next day had rang to say that her mother was critically ill in London and she would be away for a while caring for her. The Scottish Man sounded suitably sad to hear this news. No one knew better than he did that Charlotte's mother had died some years back. He wasn't concerned, Charlie had always been a worrier. He decided that she had disappeared for a while until the heat died down. *That suits me fine*, he had thought to himself and then smiled his scary smile, knowing he could find her any time he wanted to. The only other person who knew about his involvement was Fairclough. He was confident that the engineer would keep his mouth shut, he was too involved. Still no harm in giving him a last reminder. Taggert jumped up from his bed and searched his wallet for the phone number. Not finding it he thought for a moment, and then suddenly recalled that he had hidden it in the Bible, in his bedside cupboard, on top of Psalm 23, to be exact.

As soon as he opened the drawer, his heart sank. The bible was lying upside down in the centre of the drawer. He would never do that. He was too organised. He almost didn't want to look but eventually opened the Bible, to Psalm 23. As he expected, there was no piece of paper with a name and phone number written on it. He dropped the book to the floor. How could Ginger have found it, and would it mean anything to him? It didn't matter anymore. He had to assume that he was in trouble. He quickly threw his few possessions into his suitcase and briefly wondered whether he really needed to go back down into the tunnels and fetch the bag. He was almost certain that there was nothing in it that could be traced back to him, but he had started to make mistakes, he couldn't risk it. He threw the suitcase onto his bed, grabbed his keys and raced from the room.

***

The lads reluctantly strolled back to their tiny office. Dennis took one last glance at the blue sky and said.

"If we get that reward money, I'm taking Gloria to a tropical paradise, for a nice holiday."

They opened the door to the office and stared around the small room.

"Maybe we could get a bigger office as well," Stinky added, and then the phone rang.

***

The Scottish Man had raced down the stairs heading for the basement when all of a sudden, he spotted the hotel manager striding towards him.

"Oh, Mr Taggert, I've meant to come and see you. I was wondering how much longer you will need the room. How's the book coming along?"

The Scottish Man gave his most charming look.

"That's a coincidence," he said, "I was coming to see you as well. I've received an urgent phone-call, I must return home, I shall be leaving soon actually. But don't worry I have everything I need for the book. I think I can say with great confidence that the Midland Hotel and its tunnels will soon receive a great deal of publicity."

The Hotel Manager beamed.

"Don't forget, I shall require your room key and the key to the basement."

The Scottish Man held the keys in his hand.

"Of course, I shall drop them into your office. I just need to make one last quick trip down below; I think I may have left some paperwork in the basement."

Then he thanked the Hotel Manager for his valuable assistance, shook his hand and promised that he would be receiving a mention in the forward to the book. They walked off in opposite directions, neither noticing Gloria emerge from the room they had been standing next to.

***

Dennis drove as quickly as he could. Stinky glanced at the speedometer.

"Steady, Ginge, that's almost 30 miles an hour."

Dennis didn't notice the sarcasm.

"Just hold on to your seat, Stinky, we need to get there before Taggert gets away, we may catch him with the painting."

"I still think we should have rung the police," Stinky muttered.

Dennis reassured him.

"As soon as we get there, we will. If we had called from the office, Inspector Pratt might have got there before we did and claimed the credit. It's just lucky that Gloria overheard Taggert talking to the Hotel Manager."

***

The Scottish Man passed through the large basement room. In the far corner were some concrete steps and then another door. He opened that and immediately could hear the noise from the pump that pumped fresh water from the underground spring. He walked along a metal walkway. As he glanced over the railing at the side, he could look down and see the large water pump far below. He passed a large metal storage cupboard used by the maintenance men then climbed down another set of steps at the end of the walkway, and then instead of descending further to the pump. He opened another door which opened onto the first tunnel. There were dim lights on permanently in this section, enough so that he didn't need his torch. He walked about a quarter of a mile alongside the unused railway line until he came to another tunnel on his right and turned down that. Now there were no lights. He doubted if this tunnel had ever been used for anything. Long ago, something had no doubt been planned, but money had run out, a new person in charge had come up with a different plan, for whatever the reason this tunnel had never been finished. Still, luckily for the Scottish Man, before a decision had been made to cease work on this tunnel, the workers, who probably didn't realise it at the time, had reached an area just beneath the basement of the Birmingham Art Gallery and Museum. Suddenly, just in front of him, he spotted a pile of rocks at the side of the tunnel. He placed his torch on the ground to provide some light and commenced removing rocks from the pile. When he had removed enough, he reached down and pulled out a canvas bag. He picked up the torch and shone down behind the rocks. He could see smashed up pieces of wood painted gold. He threw rocks back on top of them until the remains of the frame that had once surrounded The Man from Paris with the Very Large Head were completely hidden. Then, he picked up the bag and started walking back in the direction he had come from.

Chapter 32

Dennis and Stinky ran into the foyer of The Midland Hotel and immediately spotted Gloria. She explained to them that Taggert had gone back down into the basement about fifteen minutes earlier. "I've been watching, and he hasn't returned yet, maybe it's time to call the police," she said.

Dennis held up his hand.

"Wait, maybe he's not coming back," he told her, "Maybe he knows another way out of the tunnels. He may have gone down there to pick up the painting and has no intention of coming back."

They stared at each other for a moment and then Dennis shouted.

"I'm going to fetch the torch from the car, we need to get down that tunnel and see if we can spot Taggert; once we have him with the painting in his hand, then we can involve the police. Meet me by the stairs, Stinky."

With that, he raced back out of the hotel. Gloria looked across at Stinky. Neither spoke, but they both knew what the other was thinking. Eventually, Stinky gave a slight nod of his head, and Gloria ran across the foyer.

He waited for about five minutes, watching Gloria in the phone kiosk that stood in the corner; she was talking animatedly to someone on the other end of the phone. Just as she slammed the phone down, Dennis came bursting back through the glass doors.

"Sorry," he shouted, "the torch had rolled under the car seat, took me ages to find it."

He ran to join Stinky at the stairs that led down to the basement and failed to notice Gloria emerging from the kiosk.

They raced down the steps, passed the kitchen, storerooms, laundry and finally following Gloria's directions, found the basement door. Dennis turned the doorknob, and much to his relief, the door opened. They looked around and spotted more steps at the far end of the basement, and at the bottom of these steps another door. As soon as Dennis opened this, they were hit by the noise coming from the water pump.

Stinky jumped back.

"What's that?' he asked.

"It's the water pump," Dennis told him. "It pumps water up to the hotel from an underground spring. Gloria told me all about it and the tunnels." He didn't mention it, but he suddenly wished he had paid more attention to what she had been telling him.

Inside the door was a long metal walkway, dull lights showed the way. Stinky ran and looked over the railing.

"Wow, it's a long way down," he shouted and then quickly followed his friend. As they neared the end of the walkway, Dennis suddenly held up his hand to stop his friend and pointed. Stinky looked up and saw that a large canvas bag had suddenly appeared from a hole at the side of the walkway. Next second, a hand appeared. Someone was about to emerge from below. Dennis looked around and spotted a large metal storage cupboard just ahead. He grabbed Stinky's arm and dragged him behind it. He placed the torch on the floor, looked at his friend and put a finger to his lips; then he peeped around the corner of the cupboard. The Scottish Man was just pulling himself up from the steps that led down to the tunnel. Dennis watched, as the man looked about him and then bent and picked up the bag. From the strain that showed on his face, it obviously contained something heavy. As he started to walk towards them, Dennis leapt back out of sight. Unfortunately, as he did, his foot connected with the torch lying on the ground. The boys watched in terror as it toppled over and slowly rolled out onto the walkway.

The Scottish Man struggled along the walkway carrying the bag, wondering whether he should have even bothered going back for it. *Still, no point in leaving loose ends*, he thought, *it's nearly all over.*

Then, right in front of him, something suddenly rolled from behind the metal cupboard. For a second, his mind couldn't comprehend what had happened. Then he realised it was a torch; someone was there. He didn't bother waiting to find out who, just held the bag tightly to his body and ran.

Stinky reacted the fastest.

"Quick, let's get him," he shouted and ran from behind the cupboard but then immediately slipped, and crashed onto the floor. Before he could get back up, Dennis had leapt over him and raced after Taggert.

The Scottish Man weighed down by the heavy bag glanced back over his shoulder and snarled as he saw the little ginger investigator rapidly catching up with him.

"You again," he muttered and then suddenly stopped and spun around.

Dennis was nearly upon the man. He was just wondering what he would actually do, once he caught him when the man stopped and spun around. Dennis was so close that he couldn't stop. At the last second, he saw something swinging towards him and realised it was the bag the man had been carrying. It all happened in a flash; the bag hit him in the chest, he felt all the breath being knocked out of him as he was thrown backwards. Suddenly, he hit the metal railing at the side of the walkway, and before he could do anything, he toppled over it and disappeared.

Stinky gasped. Just as he had recommenced chasing the man, he had seen him stop, turn and hit his friend with the bag, and then watched in horror as Dennis toppled over the railing. He ran toward the spot, as he did so, he saw the man run off towards the basement door. Stinky ignored him and slowly approached the railing, terrified of what he would see when he looked down below. He felt guilty; if he hadn't slipped over, he would have reached the man first. How was he going to tell Dennis's family and Gloria? He put his hands on top of the metal rail and hesitatingly leaned over the top. As he looked down, he saw a ginger head about four feet below him. Dennis had reached out as he toppled over the railing and amazingly had hung onto a water pipe that ran just below the walkway. He wasn't sure how much longer he could hang on and didn't dare look down.

When he glanced up, he suddenly saw Stinky staring down at him.

"Took your time," he gasped, "I hope you didn't stop for a sandwich."

Stinky leaned over the rail as far as he could and reached down with his right hand, but try as he might he couldn't quite reach. He could see the strain on his friends face when their eyes met.

"Please help, Stinky, I can't hold on much longer."

Stinky straightened up and said,

"Don't go anywhere, Ginge."

He looked around for some rope, anything he could use to reach his friend and then suddenly had an idea; he removed his leather belt from around his waist, wrapped one end around his right fist and then once more leaned over the railing.

Dennis stared back with terror in his eyes and then saw his friend was lowering something towards him.

"Grab the belt, Ginge," Stinky shouted.

Dennis couldn't bring himself to do it. It would mean letting go of the pipe with one hand and grabbing the belt. He didn't know if he had the strength left.

"Come on, Ginge, imagine you are back in the army doing the obstacle course," Stinky shouted.

Dennis wanted to say that he had barely managed ever to complete the obstacle course, so that wasn't helping him much, but he didn't have the energy, so he took a deep breath and let go of the pipe. For a split second, he was holding on with one hand; then he managed to grab the belt. Now, he was relying on his friend. He felt himself being pulled upwards, he looked up and could see the sweat dripping from the end of Stinky's nose.

"You need to let go with your other hand and grab my arm, Ginge," he gasped.

Dennis hesitated for a second, then he let go of the pipe and instantly grabbed his friend's arm. Stinky made one last superhuman effort and pulled him up until Dennis could reach the railing. Then he grabbed him by the arms and dragged him over the top, where he collapsed to the ground, gasping for breath.

Meanwhile, Stinky leaned against the railing; for a few minutes, neither spoke until Stinky said,

"Do you know what went through my mind as I looked down at you, Ginge?"

Dennis considered the question and then said.

"Yes, I think I do know what you what was going through your mind, Stinky. You were thinking how will I manage without my best friend, how can I possibly get through life without his help and expertise."

Stinky shook his head.

"No, nothing like that. I was just thinking that bald patch of yours is getting bigger."

Dennis dragged himself to his knees. He was just about to reply when he noticed that without his belt to hold them up, his friend's trousers had fallen down to his ankles, revealing his baggy, green, army issue underpants.

"I don't believe it," he shouted, "you were supposed to hand those underpants in when we left the army. They must be five years old, what about Rule no. 3, never leave the house without wearing clean underpants?"

Stinky looked offended.

"They are clean, Brenda washes them every Sunday."

"Well, in that case," Dennis said, "I propose an amendment to rule three: part 2, underpants need to be not only clean, but new ones should be bought every six months."

"Six months," Stinky shouted, "that's ridiculous."

But before he could argue his point, Dennis suddenly came to his senses and leapt to his feet, shouting,

"We haven't got time to discuss this now; we have a criminal to apprehend. We will discuss the underpants situation at the next monthly meeting." With that, he ran towards the basement door, closely followed by his friend. By the time Stinky reached him, he was pounding on the door.

"He's locked us down here," he shouted.

Stinky joined him, finished pulling his pants up and shouted "Help" at the top of his voice. The door immediately opened, and Gloria said,

"Your wish is my command." Then she explained how she had seen Taggert run back to his room, so she had come down to the basement looking for them.

Dennis gave her a hug and then went to move away.

"We have to stop him," he said, but Gloria grabbed his arm.

Chapter 33

"He's still there," she told him, "Inspector Pratt is talking to him now. I was worried, so I rang him and told him what was happening."

"Gloria did the right thing," Stinky added.

Dennis felt disappointed but nodded and then turned and made his way along the corridor towards the Scottish Man's room, closely followed by his friends.

When they reached his room, they spotted two police constables standing outside. One held up his hand as they approached and said.

"Run along now; this is police business."

"I need to speak to Detective Inspector Pratt," Dennis told them, so they were ordered to wait at the end of the corridor.

Dennis couldn't believe what had happened.

"Pratt's probably found the painting by now; he's going to take all the credit. That's the end of our reward money."

Then he noticed how upset Gloria looked so he added.

"It's not your fault Gloria; I know you were worried about us. I just wanted to solve the case on my own," and then he saw his friend look up, so he quickly added.

"With Stinky, of course."

Suddenly, the door to Taggert's room opened, Inspector Pratt stuck his head out, glanced up the corridor and shouted.

"You, Bisskit and Blackshaw, in here now."

They moved quickly, whilst Gloria ran to her room.

When they entered the room, Taggert was sitting on a chair looking totally relaxed. He smirked at Dennis and then when Inspector Pratt turned around the smirk left and was replaced by a look of terror.

"There they are Inspector; they are the ones who have been harassing me."

The Inspector indicated for him to be quiet and then turned to Dennis and Stinky,

"Mr Taggert has made serious allegations against you two; he claims you have been following him everywhere. You even broke into his room, and then, just now, you attacked him when he was returning from working in the tunnel."

Dennis was dumbstruck for a moment and then blurted out.

"That's ridiculous; he stole the painting from the Art Gallery."

Taggert managed to look greatly offended.

"You see, Inspector, it's exactly as I told you. I'm not sure if this man has confused me with someone else, or he is mentally deranged, but I think you can now see why I'm so worried about him."

Inspector Pratt looked from the man to Dennis and Stinky and said,

"You two better wait outside," when Dennis started to protest he added. "Now look, I only turned up here because Miss Plunkett rang me with some fanciful tale involving you two, but I am finding no evidence whatsoever of any wrongdoing by Mr Taggert, in fact, far from it, he has been most helpful and obliging."

"But what about his bag?" Stinky said, "Have you checked to see if the painting is there?"

Pratt shook his head,

"If it makes you two happy, I'll show you what's in the bag," he looked over at Taggert who nodded.

He held the bag open revealing mainly tools, hammers, chisels. Dennis's eyes lit up.

"Before you start," the inspector said. "Mr Taggert has explained these. He is writing a book on the tunnels, and part of that involves taking rock samples."

"Well, he would say that, wouldn't he?" Stinky said sarcastically.

Inspector Pratt picked up a letter off the bed and held it up.

"Here is a signed letter from Glasgow University listing Mr Taggert's qualifications. He is highly respected in his field."

"I don't doubt that," Dennis replied and then suddenly stuck a hand into the bag and pulled out a pair of gloves and then a balaclava.

Taggert stood up and angrily said.

"Oh, this is getting tiresome. I have already explained to the Inspector that it gets very cold and dusty down there. Of course, I would wear gloves and something to keep out the dust. Now, have we quite finished this charade, Inspector? I'm willing not to press any charges, just as long as they leave me in peace."

Pratt said nothing for a while and then finally made up his mind.

"I'm very sorry to have disturbed you, Mr Taggert, thank you for your cooperation." Then he turned to Dennis and Stinky and said, "Right you two, outside. I want a word with you."

He opened the door, just as Gloria approached carrying something.

"Oh, good, Miss Plunkett, you can hear this as well."

Before he could speak, Dennis shouted.

"It's him, he stole the painting, I know it."

The Inspector shook his head sadly.

"You see, that's exactly why crime investigation, should be left to the police. You amateurs just think you know who did a crime, but as professionals, we actually need to have some proof. Now if you could produce the painting, then I would be impressed."

Dennis stared despondently at the ground; if only he could. For the past few days, the whereabouts of the painting was all that he had occupied his thoughts. Gloria tapped him on the shoulder and said,

"Come on, let's go and have a cuppa."

He reluctantly followed her and Stinky down the corridor. Has he sadly glanced up, he noticed one of the hotel cleaners just up ahead. She was busy dusting a painting that hung from the wall. He slowly walked a few more steps and then stopped and stared at the ground. Stinky and Gloria turned back just as Dennis looked up and suddenly smiled.

In an instant, he had solved the case. He knew exactly where the painting was. Where else would you put a painting? He brushed past the Inspector and threw the room door wide open. Taggert, who had been waiting for them to leave, leapt to his feet and shouted.

"What now?"

Dennis ran into the room and jumped onto the bed. Inspector Pratt followed him, looking most annoyed. Dennis lifted the large painting of the tropical paradise off the wall and turned it over. Another canvas was taped to the back of it. You could only see the back, but Dennis had no doubt what it would reveal when turned over. He looked up at Taggert and saw the change in the man's expression. He suddenly ran for the open door. Inspector Pratt held up his hand, but the Scottish Man pushed him so hard in the chest, that the inspector fell over the bed. Taggert raced out of the room but failed to see Gloria standing next to the door. As he passed her, she stuck her foot out. The Scottish Man was travelling at such speed that he shot forward, head-first into the wall opposite and then slowly crumpled unconscious to the carpet.

"Nice work, Gloria," Dennis shouted as the police constables finally leapt into action and handcuffed him.

As Inspector Pratt slowly climbed to his feet, rubbing his bruised chest. Dennis carefully removed the tape from the corners of the canvas, turned it over and dropped it onto the bed and then, with a theatrical flourish said.

"Inspector Pratt, I present to you, The Man from Paris with The Very Large Head."

The Inspector and Stinky joined Dennis and stared down at the missing masterpiece. It showed a man riding a bicycle passed the Eiffel Tower; he had a black beret perched on a head, at least twice the size of a normal person. Not only that, but his right eye appeared to be above his eyebrow, and for some reason his left ear was level with his mouth.

Stinky sighed.

"I told you, utter rubbish, he can't even get the eyes in the right position. I'm no artist, but I would have thought that was just basic."

Inspector Pratt nodded his head in agreement.

"He's right, you know, it's terrible. I don't know what all the fuss is about."

Even Dennis was secretly surprised by just how bad it was but instead said,

"Well, it's not that bad, but granted it isn't one of the finest examples from his Men from Paris with Large Heads, period."

"I don't even know why it's called that," Stinky shouted. "It should be called The Horribly Mutilated Man from Paris."

"Dennis nodded,

"Quite so my friend, or, the Terribly Deformed Man from Paris, Who Also Happens to Have an Extra-Large Head, even better."

But Stinky hadn't finished.

"Or, even better than that, The Dennis Bisskit of Paris."

"Oh, very droll, Stinky, very amusing. What about, The Stinky Blackshaw's Better Looking Brother from Paris??

"Well, what about…"

But Inspector Pratt had had enough. He pushed them apart and said,

"If you two clowns have finally finished critiquing this so-called masterpiece I will take it and Mr Taggert into custody."

But Dennis jumped in between him and the painting and said,

"I think you have to agree, that even though you will have the pleasure of arresting this man, my partner and I actually solved the case for you, and I trust you will be recommending that we receive the reward money."

The Inspector looked far from happy but eventually spoke.

"Fair enough, just this once, I have to agree that you have done a good job. A lot of luck mind you, and by rights, I should be arresting you for interfering in official police business. Still, just this once, I will certainly do what I can to get you the reward, but from now on I hope you will leave crime to the police and stick to doing whatever it is you do."

Dennis lifted the canvas up, but before he could hand it over, Gloria held up the camera she had fetched from her room, shouted, "Smile," took a photo and added, "Just in case you forget Inspector."

The photograph, showing a smiling Dennis and Stinky, standing either side of the painting, was the one that appeared on the front page of the following week's newspaper, under the heading.

"LOCAL PRIVATE INVESTIGATORS SOLVE MYSTERY OF MISSING MASTERPIECE."

Part 5

Chapter 34

3 AM, 21st July 1969

Stinky woke with a start and leapt to his feet.

"Did I miss anything?"

Dennis was staring at his reflection in the mirror on the lounge wall but muttered,

"You just missed Cilla Black singing."

Stinky rubbed his eyes.

"No, I mean has anyone emerged from the spaceship yet?"

Dennis shook his head.

"I wish they would get on with it. If I'd landed on the moon, I would want to get out and have a look around, straight away."

Stinky took a sip from his mug of tea and then pulled a face.

"Tea's gone cold," he mumbled and then added. "I suppose they are having a good look outside the window first, just to make sure there are no little green men about."

He waited for Dennis to reply but then noticed he was licking his fingers and flattening down some flyaway strands of hair.

"You do realise, Ginge, that you can now afford to buy a little ginger toupee."

Dennis turned to look at his friend.

"No need for that, Stinky. If you look carefully, you will see there is already a considerable sign of regrowth. I didn't tell you before, but I have been using Granddad's special homemade hair-restorer. It's his own invention, a combination of duck poo and vinegar and it definitely seems to be working."

"Oh, that explains it," Stinky said, "I was wondering what the smell was."

"Well, it's a small price to pay," Dennis told him.

Stinky nodded.

"There is one small point that you appear to have overlooked, and that's that for as long as I've known your granddad, he hasn't had a hair on his head."

"Well, of course, he hasn't," Dennis said, "that's because he stopped using the duck poo and vinegar. He said you get to a certain age and it's not worth bothering anymore."

Stinky looked at the small television set in the corner. Though it was a grainy black and white picture, he could easily make out the spacecraft, sitting on the surface of the moon.

He still couldn't quite believe it. So much had happened in the last few weeks.

They had not only received the five-thousand-pound reward money but, because of all the publicity, they had been inundated with work. They had finally moved to a bigger office, which was large enough for them and their clients to sit in at the same time. Stinky had bought a new car so Dennis didn't have to chauffeur him around everywhere and they hadn't forgotten others who'd assisted them. Dennis had presented Dawkins with a season ticket to the cricket and Stinky had given Jane Fonda, the cleaning lady, an envelope containing fifty pounds. She had cried tears of joy and said it was the most money she had ever seen; then she had made Stinky promise to drop into The Red Lion one evening for a sing-song with her and her friend.

"So, Ginge, if you are not spending your money on a little ginger toupee, what are you going to spend it on?"

Dennis thought for a moment and then replied.

"Well, first of all, I am taking Gloria away on holiday."

Stinky held a hand up.

"Hang on, let me guess. Fiji, Honolulu, Tahiti?"

Dennis interrupted him.

"Blackpool. Mrs Muggin's B&B, full English breakfast, including black pudding and free entry into the Bingo Hall next door."

"Sounds exotic," Stinky said, "but what happened to the tropical paradise you were anxious to see?"

Dennis looked shocked.

"I don't know whatever gave you that idea, my friend. I learnt my lesson years ago when I visited France with Granddad; you can only get a decent cup of tea in England."

Just then, the kitchen door flew open, and the girls came in carrying trays of sandwiches and biscuits, and a pot of tea.

"Any signs of life yet?" Brenda shouted.

Stinky shook his head.

"Nothing, no astronauts and no Martians."

"Well, strictly speaking," Dennis told him, "Martians are from Mars. On the moon, you would get…" he thought for a moment and then said, "Moonians."

Gloria poured them a fresh, hot cup of tea and they filled plates with food.

Stinky raised his cup and said,

"I would like to propose a toast. It's been a momentous year for us all, and now we are together to watch a momentous time for the world. I can't think of anyone I would rather share it with."

They all raised the cups, and then Dennis stood up and said,

"That's reminded me, I have an important announcement to make."

He reached into his pocket and pulled out a small card.

"In recognition of Stin… I mean Jack's tremendous bravery, in risking his own life to save mine when we were down in the Birmingham tunnel. I have decided to change the name of the agency to the one he always wanted." He held the card up so everyone could read it.

"DOUBLE B PRIVATE INVESTIGATORS"

Brenda glanced at Gloria, and they both started laughing.

"It sounds like a bra size," Gloria eventually gasped.

Dennis groaned.

"See, that's exactly what I told you. Right, forget all about that, we are back to being, BISSKIT AND BLACKSHAW PRIVATE INVESTIGATORS."

Stinky quickly grabbed the card and placed it in his pocket.

"I'm keeping that," he said. "One day I'll be able to show it to my grandchildren and say, 'For a couple of seconds, I got my own way over Dennis Bisskit.'"

But Dennis wasn't listening; he'd noticed that the moon and spaceship had disappeared. He got up and picked up the antenna sitting on top of the television. He walked around the room, and eventually a blurred picture appeared; an astronaut was awkwardly climbing down the steps of the spaceship.

"That's it," Gloria shouted, "Don't move, Dennis."

Dennis tried to look over his shoulder so that he could witness what was happening, but every time he moved the picture disappeared, and everyone shouted at him, which explained why Dennis Bisskit, despite staying up half of the night, came to miss man's historical first steps upon the moon. All he heard was the awestruck silence of his friends and eventually a distant voice proclaiming, "That's one small step for man, one giant leap for mankind."

Eventually, Dennis's arm grew tired, he placed the antenna back upon the television set and sat back down on his chair.

"I still can't believe that our friend, The Professor, predicted that man would walk on the moon before the end of the decade, nearly ten years ago," Stinky said.

"What about you, Jack, what did you predict?" Brenda enquired.

Stinky shook his head.

"I can't remember, but I do know that Dennis predicted that the Davy Crockett hat would be even more popular than the Trilby by the end of the decade."

They all laughed, especially Gloria who managed to snort her mouthful of tea out of her nose.

"You may laugh," Dennis told them, "but the decade is not over yet, there is still time for my prediction to come true, and you may have forgotten what you said, Stinky, I mean Jack," he quickly corrected before Brenda shouted at him, "but I can still recall it; you said that before the end of the decade, you would be married to the most beautiful girl in Dudley. We asked you who that was, but you wouldn't say, but later, when we were alone in our tent, you told me that you had been to see The Man from Sherwood Forest, with a certain Miss Brenda Rumble, and one day she would be your wife."

Brenda stood up with tears in her eyes.

"Oh Jack, you never told me that. That's just wonderful."

She rushed over and gave him a big hug, but Dennis wasn't finished.

"Well I'm glad that you're happy, Brenda, but I certainly wasn't. He had promised to see the Man from Sherwood Forest with me. In the end, I had to go with Billy Flynn, he of the famous wedding speech. I couldn't hear anything; no one makes as much noise eating a bucket of popcorn as Billy does."

They laughed again and then Gloria said.

"Well, don't worry, Dennis, from now on you can take me to the movies, on one condition, that is. You really must get some new shampoo, that one smells like a combination of duck poo and vinegar."

Dennis glanced over at Stinky who looked like he was just about to make a comment when Brenda suddenly leapt to her feet and raced back into the kitchen. Seconds later, she came back shouting.

"I nearly forgot the most important thing."

She placed a large chocolate cake on the table. On top, in white icing, she had made a replica of the moon with a little rocket heading towards it. They all cheered. Dennis excused himself to go to the toilet. Brenda cut them all a large slice then put her plate on the floor next to her chair whilst she popped back into the kitchen to get more milk. Seconds later, Dennis strode back into the room. Failing to notice Brenda's plate full of chocolate cake on the floor, he placed a foot squarely in the centre of it. The plate slid along the shiny floor until Dennis had nearly done the splits, then he toppled over backwards, crashing into the table. A couple of table legs snapped off, and as the table fell forwards, the remains of the chocolate cake slid down and landed on top of Dennis's head.

For a few seconds, no one spoke and then Stinky and Gloria fell to their knees, tears rolling down their cheeks, even Dennis joined in as cake slid down his face.

Brenda raced in from the kitchen and stared horrified at the destruction Dennis had managed to achieve in the few moments that she had been away.

"What have you done?" she screamed. Stinky answered for him

"The Neil Armstrong of Dudley just took one giant leap for mankind, straight into your chocolate cake."

209

Dennis wiped some cake from his nose, stuck it into his mouth and said, "Mmm! Lovely cake Brenda," and eventually she could stay angry no more and joined her friends in their joy and laughter.

Epilogue
October 1969

Stinky ran up the steps and along the corridor. Outside the office door, he could see one pair of shoes, Dennis's.

He opened the door and as usual contemplated whether he should invest in a pair of sunglasses. Not only were the walls of the new office painted white, but Dennis had insisted on having the floor covered in a dazzling white carpet. It had caused long arguments. Evidently, Dennis had seen a movie in which the detective had a similarly carpeted office. "It looked classy," he'd said. Stinky had told him it was a stupid idea, and it was only a matter of time before it got wrecked, and you should always buy carpets the same colour as dirt, then you didn't have to clean them. As usual, Dennis had had the final say, and now, they lived in constant fear of damaging it. Anyone entering the office had to leave their shoes outside. The other day when several people had visited, it had looked like someone was opening a shoe shop in the corridor. Every morning, they would spend several minutes on their hands and knees checking for spots.

Dennis was chatting with someone on the brand new white telephone and looking very pleased with himself.

Suddenly, he said his goodbyes and put the receiver down.

"Good news, Stinky, more work; a Mr Goldstein is transporting some diamonds to London. He doesn't like to use security firms, and he needs someone to escort him, he needs a bodyguard."

Stinky nodded.

"Sounds okay, if the money's good. I can do that."

Dennis looked astounded.

"Oh, no, no, no, Stinky. No offence. I know you can look after yourself, but this job calls for a man with special qualifications, a man trained in the martial arts."

Stinky stared back, trying to think of someone they knew who was trained in the martial arts.

"You seem to be forgetting my karate training, my friend. You may not know it, but in some places, I am known as the Karate Master of Dudley."

Stinky couldn't believe it.

"Well, as I recall it, you actually attended one karate class. You injured your hand, trying to snap a small length of Balsa wood and vowed never to go back again. So, I'm guessing that these places where you are evidently known as the Karate Master of Dudley, are the type of places where people live, who have absolutely no concept of what the word karate actually means."

Dennis ignored him, stood up and removed his white jacket.

"Give me room, Stinky; I must practise my karate moves." He moved from behind his desk and balanced on one foot whilst seemingly attempting to kick an imaginary target with his other foot.

"In that case, I'm going to go and grab a mug of tea, Ginge, try not to injure yourself whilst I'm away."

As he left the office, the telephone rang just as Dennis had his right leg raised. He toppled over, crashing into the desk. Stinky left him to it.

Five minutes later, he returned with his mug of tea, removed his shoes and opened the door. Dennis was still holding the phone, he had a strange expression on his face and for once was doing the listening, rather than the talking. Stinky glanced over at the framed manuscript on the wall, headed:

BISSKIT AND BLACKSHAW PRIVATE INVESTIGATORS
RULES AND REGULATIONS.

As usual, he paid special attention to,
RULE 3...INVESTIGATORS MUST NEVER LEAVE THE HOUSE WITHOUT CLEAN UNDERPANTS and then underneath it, the amendment.
PART 2...ALL OLD UNDERPANTS MUST BE DISCARDED AND NEW ONES PURCHASED EVERY SIX MONTHS.
Stinky had finally agreed to it, but he had drawn the line at Dennis's request, for an amendment to the amendment, monthly

underpants inspections. The way he saw it was what Dennis didn't know, couldn't worry him, and Stinky was fairly confident that he still had at least a good couple of years left in his old army issue underpants.

He suddenly realised that Dennis hadn't said a word since he had entered the room. Finally, he muttered, "Thank you for letting us know," put the phone down and stood up.

"That was Inspector Pratt," he told Stinky, "Evidently, Taggert was in court today for a hearing."

Stinky nodded.

"I know, I read it in the paper."

But Dennis continued as if he hadn't heard him.

"For the last couple of days, he'd complained of stomach troubles. When they arrived at the court, he'd started groaning and clutching his stomach and said he had to use the toilet. A police constable locked him in and stood guard outside. After five minutes, he knocked to see what was keeping him and got no reply. Eventually, they kicked the door down; the toilet was empty; somehow he'd opened the locked window and got out, even though they were on the third floor."

Stinky just stood there with his mug of tea in his hand and his mouth open, as if he didn't quite understand what Dennis was saying.

"He's gone, Stinky, the Scottish Man, has escaped."

After a few seconds, the mug slipped from Stinky's grasp and fell to the ground. Amazingly, it didn't shatter; in fact, it landed the right way up. Unfortunately, the contents shot into the air and then gently showered back down onto the white carpet.

They both stared at the mess that had once been Dennis's pride and joy until finally, Stinky said,

"I told you, we should never have bought a white carpet."

THE END

213